On a certain night Rona Durant decided to leave her husband . . .

On a certain night Jerry Durant decided to leave Rona Durant, his wife . . .

Rona picked up her suitcase. Just simple things she'd need. A few clothes, a *lot* of credit cards. Her jewelry case. Also she packed a stuffed toy penguin with a yellow rubber beak that glowed in the dark . . .

In his bedroom (formerly the guestroom), Jerry Durant packed a suitcase. Bare necessities. A few bottles of scotch. The plaid sports jacket Rona hated. Then he looked around for a stuffed toy penguin with a yellow rubber beak that glowed in the dark . . .

The stuffed toy penguin was gone!

WHAT KIND OF FILTHY SNEAKING LOWLIFE SLIME WOULD KIDNAP A STUFFED TOY PENGUIN WITH A YELLOW RUBBER BEAK THAT GLOWS IN THE DARK?
—From "Your Penguin or Mine?" by Bruce Scates

MYSTERIOUS MENAGERIE

Edited by
Cynthia Manson

BERKLEY PRIME CRIME, NEW YORK

MYSTERIOUS MENAGERIE

A Berkley Prime Crime Book / published by arrangement with
Dell Magazines, a division of Bantam Doubleday Dell, Inc.

PRINTING HISTORY
Berkley Prime Crime edition / March 1996

The Putnam Berkley World Wide Web site address is
http://www.berkley.com

ISBN: 0-425-15232-4

Berkley Prime Crime Books are published
by The Berkley Publishing Group,
200 Madison Avenue, New York, NY 10016.
The name BERKLEY PRIME CRIME and the
BERKLEY PRIME CRIME design
are trademarks belonging to Berkley Publishing Corporation.

PRINTED IN THE UNITED STATES OF AMERICA

10 9 8 7 6 5 4 3 2 1

CONTENTS

INTRODUCTION

Mysterious Menagerie, as the title suggests, is an anthology of mystery stories featuring a wide variety of animals in leading or supporting roles. Although there have been several cat and dog anthologies published, it is likely that mystery fans will find themselves absorbed in stories where a wide range of animals play key roles. For those traditional cat and dog lovers, we have an unusual cat story by Lilian Jackson Braun as well as a lighthearted dog story by Penelope Wallace.

However, for those of you animal lovers whose taste runs to the more exotic, we have everything from kangaroos to penguins, elephants to buffalo. For those mystery fans who need a quick scare, we have tigers, bears, and snakes. So, take cover.

In addition to this wonderful array of mystery stories that are sometimes amusing, more often frightening, we have a strong lineup of well-known authors. Such talent includes the works of P. G. Wodehouse, G. K. Chesterton, Isaac Asimov, Loren D. Estleman, and Clark Howard. So sit back, find yourself a pet to keep you company, and enjoy this entertaining collection of mystery stories where a dog is not always "man's best friend."

—Cynthia Manson

STANLEY AND SPOOK

LILIAN JACKSON BRAUN

When I first met Jane she used to say: "I'd rather have kittens than kids." Then years later she had one of each: Stanley and Spook, a most unusual pair. She also had a successful engineer for a husband and a lovely house in the Chicago suburbs and a new car every year.

In the interim we had kept in touch, more or less, by means of Christmas cards and vacation postcards. Then one spring I attended a business conference in Chicago and telephoned Jane to say hello.

She was elated! "Linda, you've got to come out here for a visit when you've finished with your meetings. Ed has an engineering job in Saudi Arabia, and I'm here alone with Stanley and Spook. I'd love to have you meet them. And you and I can talk about old times."

She gave me directions. "When you get off the freeway, go four miles north, then take a left at the cider mill until you come to Maplewood Farms. It's a winding road. We're the last house—white with black shutters and an *enormous* maple tree in front. You can't miss it."

Late Friday afternoon I rented a car and drove to the affluent suburbs, recalling that we had once lived contentedly in tents. Now Jane lived in Maplewood Farms, and I had an apartment with a view on New York's Upper East Side.

When Jane and I first met, we were newly married to a pair of young engineers who were building a dam in the northern wilderness. The first summer, we lived in a sprawling "tent city" and thought it a great adventure. After all, we were young and still had rice in our hair. Eventually, cottages were built for the engineers. *Shacks* would be a better description. Jane decorated hers, I remember, with pictures of cats, and for Christmas Ed gave her an amber Persian that she named Maple Sugar. That's when she made her memorable announcement about kittens and kids. All that seemed ages ago.

Arriving at Maplewood Farms, I was driving slowly down the winding avenue admiring the well landscaped houses when I noticed a fire truck at the far end. People were grouped on the lawns and the pavement, watching, but there was no sign of anxiety. Actually, everyone seemed quite happy.

I parked and approached two couples who were standing in the middle of the street, sipping cocktails. "What's happening?" I asked.

A woman in a Moroccan caftan smiled and said: "Spook climbed up the big maple and doesn't know how to get down."

"Third time this month," said a man in an embroidered Mexican shirt. "Up go our taxes!—Would you like a drink, honey?"

The other man suggested: "Why don't they cut down the tree?"

"Or put Spook on a leash," the first woman said. Everyone laughed.

The fire truck had extended its ladder high into the branches of the big maple, and I watched as a fireman climbed up and disappeared into the leafy green. A moment or two later, he came back into view and a cheer went up from the bystanders. He was carrying a small boy in jeans and a Chicago Cubs sweatshirt.

Jane, waiting at the foot of the ladder, hugged and scolded the child—an adorable six-year-old with his father's blond hair and his mother's big brown eyes. Then she and I had a tearful, happy reunion.

"I thought Spook was your *cat*," I said.

"No, *Stanley* is the cat," Jane explained. "There he is on the front step. He's dying to meet you."

Stanley was a big, gorgeous feline with thick blond fur and a spotless white bib. He followed us into the house, his plumed tail waving with authority and aplomb.

Jane instructed her son: "Show Aunt Linda to the guest room and then bring her out to the deck for cocktails."

Spook lugged my overnight case upstairs and showed a great deal of curiosity about its contents when I unpacked. "Are you my aunt?" he wanted to know.

"Not really. But you can call me Aunt Linda. I'd like that."

Then the four of us assembled on the redwood deck overlooking a flawless lawn and a wooded ravine, its edge dotted with clumps of jonquils. Jane and Stanley and I made ourselves comfortable on the cushioned wrought-iron chairs, while Spook—now wearing a camouflage jumpsuit—chose to sit on the Indian grass rug at my feet. He was an affectionate little boy and his Buster Brown haircut was charming. He leaned against my legs in a possessive way, and when I rumpled his hair he looked up and smiled happily, then licked his fingers and straightened his blond bangs. I thought to myself, He's as vain as his good-looking father.

As we sipped orange juice and vodka, I asked how Spook got his name.

"He's really Ed Junior," Jane said, "but he was born on Halloween and Ed called him Spook. At school the teacher insists on calling him Edward, but he's Spook to all the neighbors.— Linda, you're the perfect image of a successful young woman executive, just like the pictures in the magazines. I envy you."

Spook said: "Are you a lady engineer?"

"No, I'm an industrial electronic-supplies sales manager."

"Oh," he said, and after a moment added: "Is that hard to do?"

"Not if you like Zener diodes and unijunction transistors."

"Oh," he said, and then he climbed onto my lap.

"Spook dear," his mother admonished, "always ask permission before sitting on laps."

"That's all right," I assured her. "I like little boys."

"He loves to be petted."

"Don't we all? How long will Ed be gone, Jane?"

"Another three weeks."

"Don't you mind his long absences?"

She hesitated. "Yes—but it's a good living. It's paying for a housekeeper five days a week and a good college for Spook and some fabulous vacations."

As we talked, the cat listened, turning his head to watch each of us as we spoke. "Stanley looks so intelligent," I remarked.

"He's good company. He's almost human.—Linda, you never told me why you and Bill divorced."

"I wanted a career of my own," I said. "I was tired of being a dam-builder's wife. The construction camp was driving me up the wall and Bill was drinking heavily. Things were all wrong."

At this point a robin flew into the yard and tugged at a worm, alerting Spook, who jumped from my lap and chased him. The crafty bird took flying hops just lengthy enough to stay beyond the boy's grasp.

"That robin comes every evening during the cocktail hour," Jane said. "He likes to tease Spook, I think. Stanley isn't the slightest bit interested."

"Are you going to have any more children, Jane?"

"We'd like to adopt a girl. After what I went through with Spook, I couldn't face childbirth again. He was born at the camp, you know—a year or two after you left. I didn't have proper prenatal care because I refused to go to that so-called doctor at the camp. Do you remember him?"

I nodded. "His office smelled more of whiskey than antiseptic."

"He made passes at everybody, and I do mean *everybody!*"

"They couldn't get a really good doctor to go up there and live in those conditions." At that moment a large dog bounded over a fence and headed straight for the boy. Spook had been lying on the lawn, chewing a blade of grass, but he scrambled to his feet and headed for the nearest tree. "Spook, no more climbing, *please!*" his mother called. "Juneau won't hurt you. She just wants to play."

The man in the Mexican shirt came to the fence, calling: "Here, Juneau. Come on home, baby." To us he explained: "She broke her chain again. Sorry."

Precisely as we finished our second drink, Stanley jumped

down from his chair with a fifteen-pound *thump* and went to Jane, putting one paw on her knee.

"Stanley's telling me it's time for dinner," she said. "Linda, I'll put the ramekins in the microwave while I'm feeding the cat. Mrs. Phipps fixed chicken divan for us before she left. You might see if you can find the son-and-heir and tell him it's time to wash up."

I wandered around the grounds, noting the professionally perfect flower beds, until I found Spook. He was digging among the jonquils. "What are you doing?" I asked.

"Digging," he said.

"You're getting your jumpsuit all muddy. Come and clean up. It's time for dinner."

He raised his nose and sniffed. "Chicken!" he squealed, and headed for the house, running in joyful circles as he went. A few minutes later he appeared at the dinner table, looking spic and span in chinos and a tiger-striped knit shirt, with his face and hands scrubbed and his Buster Brown haircut combed to perfection.

We dined at a table on the deck. Stanley tried to leap onto the redwood railing nearby, but he missed his footing and fell to the floor, landing on his back.

"Honestly, he's the most awkward cat I've ever seen," Jane muttered. "Come on, Stanley. Aunt Linda won't mind if you sit with us at the table." She indicated the fourth chair, and he lumbered up onto the seat, where he sat tall and attentively. She said: "Stanley's mother was Maple Sugar. Do you remember her, Linda? She had a litter of five kittens, but he was the only one who survived. He's a little odd, but isn't he a beaut?"

Spook was picking chunks of chicken out of his ramekin and gobbling them hungrily.

"Don't forget the broccoli, dear," his mother said. "It makes little boys grow big and strong. Did you tell Aunt Linda you're going to take swimming lessons?"

"I don't want to take swimming lessons," he announced.

"It will be fun, dear. And someday you might be a champion swimmer, just like Daddy before his accident."

"I don't want to take swimming lessons," he repeated, and he scratched his ear vigorously.

"Not at the table, *please*," his mother corrected him.

To change the touchy subject I asked: "What do you like to do best, Spook?"

"Go to the zoo," he said promptly.

"Do you have any favorite animals?"

"Lions and tigers!" His eyes sparkled.

"That reminds me!" I said. Excusing myself, I ran upstairs for the gifts I had brought: a designer scarf for Jane, a cap for Spook with a furry tiger-head on top. My gift for Stanley—a plastic ball with a bell inside—seemed ridiculously inappropriate for the sedate cat. A videotape of Shakespearean readings might have been more to his taste, I told myself.

After Spook had been put to bed, Jane and I spent the evening chatting in the family room, accompanied—of course—by Stanley. Jane talked about her volunteer work and country-club life and Ed's engineering projects around the globe. I talked (boringly perhaps) about thyratrons and ignitrons and linear variable differential transformers. Stanley listened intently, putting in an occasional profound "mew."

I said: "He reminds me of a Supreme Court justice or a distinguished prime minister. How old is he?"

"Same age as Spook. They say a year of a cat's life is equivalent to seven in a human, so he's really forty-two going on forty-nine. He and Spook were born on the same day, and we always have a joint birthday party. I never told you about Spook's birth, did I? It's a miracle I lived through it.—Let's have a nightcap and I'll tell you."

She poured sherry and then went on: "Ed intended to have me airlifted to a hospital when my time came, but Spook was three weeks early, and Ed was away—hiring some more construction workers. The doctor was on one of his legendary binges and I refused to go to the infirmary, it was so crude. The boss's wife and a woman from Personnel were with me, but I was screaming and moaning and they were frantic. Finally the sheriff brought a midwife from the nearest town—and then I really did scream! All she needed was a broomstick and a tall black hat. At first I thought she was wearing a Halloween mask!"

"Oh, lord!" I said. "They sent you Cora! Cora Sykes or Sypes or something. She took care of me when I had that terrible swamp fever, and I think she tried to poison me."

"She was an evil woman. She hated everyone connected with the dam."

"It's no wonder she was bitter," I said in Cora's defense. "Her farm was due to be flooded when the dam was completed. She was forcibly removed from the house where she had lived all her life."

Jane looked pensive. "Do you believe in witchcraft, Linda?"

"Not really."

"There was a lot of gossip about that woman after you left the camp. She said—in fact, she boasted—that her ancestors had lived in Salem, Massachusetts. Does that ring a bell?— She told several people that she'd put a curse on the dam."

"I heard about that."

"It looked to me as if the curse was working. After Ed's horrible accident there was a string of peculiar mishaps and an epidemic of some kind. And I never told you this, Linda, but Spook was born blind."

"Jane! I didn't know that! But he's all right now, isn't he?"

"Yes, he's okay, but it gave us a bad scare for a while."

We talked on and on, until I remembered that I had to catch an early plane in the morning.

After I went to bed, I felt uneasy. Maplewood Farms and the dam-building experience were so far removed from my familiar world of tachometer generators and standard interface modules that I longed to return to New York. There was something unsettling, as well, about the boy and the cat. It was a situation I wanted to analyze later, when my perspective would be sharper. At the moment, exhaustion at the end of a busy week was putting me to sleep.

At some unthinkably early hour, my slumber was disturbed by a strange sensation. Before opening my eyes I tried to identify it, tried to remember where I was. Not in my New York apartment. Not in a Chicago hotel. I was at Maplewood Farms, and Spook was licking my face!

I jumped to a sitting position.

"Mommy wants to know—eggs or French toast?" he recited carefully.

"Thank you, Spook, but all I want is a roll and coffee. It's too early for anything more."

Frankly, I was glad to say goodbye and head for the airport. The situation at Maplewood Farms was too uncomfortably weird. I dared not think about it while I was driving. After I had boarded the plane and fortified myself with a Bloody Mary, however, I tackled the puzzle of Spook's tree-climbing, bird-stalking, and face-licking. He did everything but purr! Could Jane's inordinate fondness for cats have imprinted her son in some—*spooky* way?

Everything added up. I recalled the way the boy rubbed his head against me when he was pleased, smiling and squeezing his eyes shut. He was afraid of dogs. He was reluctant to swim. At the zoo his preference was for the big cats. He was always licking his fingers to smooth his hair. Then I remembered something else: like a kitten, he had been born blind! I shuddered involuntarily and ordered another Bloody Mary.

While the boy had so many catly traits, Stanley had none at all. How could one explain the situation? Well—they had been born on the same day, they had been born in the same cottage. For both mothers—Jane and Maple Sugar—it had been a difficult birth. And that disagreeable woman—Cora What's-her-name—had been in charge.

Other old friends from the construction camp had told me about Cora's curse on the dam, and although I don't believe such nonsense I had to admit that the project and all those connected with it had suffered a run of bad luck. My marriage broke up, and Bill became an alcoholic. Jane's vain, handsome, athletic husband lost a leg in a bulldozer rollover. Other men were crushed under falling trees or buried in mudslides. And, ironically, the dam was never completed.

After lives were lost and the environment was desecrated and billions of dollars were spent, the dam was abandoned. They blamed it on political pressure, cost overruns, a new administration in Washington—everything. Now I began to wonder. Was there some truth in what they said about Cora? When she was brought to the camp to nurse me during my fever, she was always moving her lips soundlessly. Was she muttering incantations under her breath?

Could she have cast some kind of spell on the two newborn creatures? Would it be possible to transpose the personality traits of the boy and the cat? Transpose their souls, so to speak? I know more about thyratrons and ignitrons than about souls, but the notion was tantalizing. At thirty-two thousand feet, it's easy to fantasize.

That was in early June. I wrote my thank-you note to Jane and in August received a postcard from Alaska. She and Ed were showing Spook the icebergs and polar bears, but he was fascinated chiefly by the puffin birds.

Then in December the usual expensive Christmas card arrived, with a brief note enclosed.

"Dear Linda: Sad news! My dear Stanley was run over by a bakery truck on Halloween. It was delivering a birthday cake for him and Spook. There will never be another cat like Stanley. I still miss him.

"Otherwise we are well. Spook is seven now and turning into a real boy. He's stopped ear scratching and people licking and other childish habits that you probably noticed when you were here. He's taking swimming lessons at the clubhouse and he wants a dog for Christmas. I suppose he was just going through a phase. Love, Jane."

My speculations were right! The mix-up was conjured by that bitter, hateful woman at the construction camp. And Stanley's death—in some mysterious way—had broken the spell.

THE PLATEAU

CLARK HOWARD

Tank Sherman felt his daughter's hand shaking him gently. "Tank. Tank, wake up. Bruno's dead."

Tank sat up, moving his legs off the side of the cot where he had been napping, fully clothed except for his boots. Bruno? Bruno dead?

"You mean Hannah," he said, automatically reaching for his boots.

"No, Tank, I mean Bruno. Hannah's still alive. It's Bruno that died."

Tank frowned. That was not the way it was supposed to happen. He pushed first one foot, then the other, into black Atlas boots with riding heels. He had owned the boots for eighteen years, and they were as soft as glove leather. After he got them on, he sat staring at the floor, still confused. Bruno dead? How could that be? Bruno was supposed to have survived Hannah. Bruno was young; Hannah was old. And it was on Bruno that the lottery had been held.

"What happened?" he asked Delia, his daughter.

"I don't know. Doc Lewis is on his way over to check him." She crossed the little one-room cabin to the stove and turned on a burner under the coffee pot. Getting out a cup, she poured a shot of peach brandy into it. "Will they still have the hunt, do you think? Since it's Hannah and not Bruno?"

"No," Tank said emphatically, "they couldn't. Hannah's too old. It wouldn't be a hunt; it would be a target shoot."

When the coffee was ready, Delia poured it in with the brandy and brought it to him. As he sipped it, Tank studied his daughter. She had the dark hair of her mother: thick and black as a crow's wing. And the high cheekbones of her mother's people, the Shoshone. Her light halfbreed coloring and blue eyes she got from him. All her life she had called him "Tank" instead of "Daddy." At nineteen, her body was round and strong. She lived in her own mobile home down the road, and dealt blackjack for a living in an illegal game behind the Custer's Last Stand restaurant. Tank himself still lived in the cabin where Delia had been born. He had been alone for a year, since Delia left; and lonely for six years, since her mother had died of bone disease.

"Are you going down to the concession?" Delia asked.

"In a minute." He held the coffee cup with both hands, as if warming his palms, and smiled at his daughter. "Remember how your Ma used to raise hell when she caught you lacing my coffee with brandy?"

"Yes." Delia smiled back.

"She always wanted me to make something of myself, your Ma. Always wanted me to do something important. But I guess it just isn't in the cards. If Hannah had died first, like she was supposed to, why, I could have done something important for the first time in my life. Important to your Ma, at least. And to Bruno. But Bruno ups and dies first, so I'm left with nothing important to do. If your Ma was still alive, she'd swear on her medicine bag that I arranged it this way."

Shaking his head wryly, Tank drank a long swallow from his cup. At fifty, he was a rangy, well worn man with not an ounce of fat on him. His face showed the results of a hundred fists, maybe more. Twenty years earlier he had come to town as part of a traveling boxing show, whites against Indians. Dan Sherman, his name had been, but they billed him as "Tank" because he was so tough. Tank Sherman, after the Sherman tank. A hide like armor. Took punches like Jake LaMotta. But he had taken too many by then. In their little Montana town, a Northern Cheyenne who hated whites had beaten him to a pulp, and when the outfit moved on it took the Northern Cheyenne with it and left Tank behind. Delia's mother had found him sitting behind the 7-Eleven, trying to eat some crackers and Vienna sausage he had bought with his last dollar. His lips were swollen so grotesquely he could barely chew, his eyes puffed to slits through which he could hardly see. Delia's mother took him home with her. They were never to part. Delia was their only child.

"Let's go on down to the concession," Tank said when he finished his coffee.

His cabin was on the slope of a low hill, and as Tank and Delia walked down its path they could see a small crowd already beginning to gather at the concession's corral. The concession itself was nothing more than a small barn next to the corral, with a gaudy red sign over its door which read: LAST TWO LIVING BUFFALO—ADMISSION $1. Tourists bought tickets and lined up around the corral, then the barn doors were opened and Bruno and Hannah were driven out to be viewed. They were the last two remaining buffalo in North America.

Now there was only one.

Old Doc Lewis, the reservation veterinarian from the nearby Crow agency, had just finished examining Bruno when Tank and Delia eased their way through the crowd to him.

"What killed him, Doc?" asked Tank, looking down at the great mass of animal spread out on the ground.

"Stroke," the vet said, brushing off his knees. "He was carrying too much weight. Must have been upwards of two thousand pounds."

Tank nodded. "Can't run off much fat in a corral," he observed.

Doc Lewis was making notes in a small book. "How old was he, do you know?"

"Nine," Tank said. "My wife helped deliver him." His scarred boxer's face saddened as he noticed his daughter reach out and pat the dead buffalo's massive head. Then he glanced over to a corner of the corral and saw Hannah, standing quietly, watching. Unlike Bruno, a young bull, Hannah was a cow and much older: at least thirty. She had thinner, lighter hair than most buffalo, and a triangular part of her neck and shoulder cape was almost blonde, indicating the presence somewhere in her ancestry of a white buffalo. Much smaller than

Bruno, she stood only five feet at her shoulders and weighed a shade over seven hundred pounds.

"I guess this means the big hunt is off, doesn't it, Doc?" Tank asked. It was the same question Delia had asked him, and Doc gave the same answer.

"Of course. There wouldn't be any sport at all going after Hannah. She's much too old."

The three of them walked over to Hannah and, as if compelled by some irresistible urge, they all patted her at once. "Well, old girl," Doc said, "you made the history books. The last North American plains buffalo."

"Maybe they'll put her on a stamp or something," said Delia.

"Maybe," Doc allowed. "They already had the buffalo on a nickel, but that was before your time."

From the barn, a pretty young woman in the tan uniform of a state park ranger walked over to them. White, educated, poised, she was everything Delia was not. "Hello, Dr. Lewis— Mr. Sherman," she said. "Hello there, Delia." She snapped a lead rein onto the collar Hannah wore. "I just got a call from headquarters to close down the concession. And to trim Hannah's hooves. Isn't it exciting?"

Doc and Tank exchanged surprised looks. "Isn't what exciting?" Doc asked, almost hesitantly. Instinctively, both he and Tank already knew what her answer would be.

"The hunt, of course. Oh, I know it won't be the same as it would have been with Bruno as the prey. But it will still be the last buffalo hunt ever. That's history in the making!"

"That," Doc rebuked, "is barbarism."

"Are you saying the hunt's still on?" Tank asked. "With Hannah as the prey?"

"Of course." She shrugged her pretty shoulders. "I mean, how else can it be? The tickets have been sold, the lottery has been held. You don't expect the state to go back on its word, do you?"

"No," Delia said, "definitely not. Never. Not the state."

"Well, there you are," the young ranger said, missing Delia's sarcasm entirely. "But, listen, they *have* changed the rules a little to make it fairer. Bruno was only going to be given a twelve-hour start, remember? Well, Hannah gets a full *twenty-four*." She smiled, apparently delighted by the allowance.

Doc Lewis turned and walked away, thoroughly disgusted. Tank and Delia left also. Walking back up the path to Tank's cabin, Delia said, "Looks like you're getting your chance to do something important, after all."

Tank, thinking about his dead wife, nodded. "Looks like . . ."

When it had become clear that the plains buffalo had finally reached the threshold of extinction, when it was absolutely certain that no new calves would be born because the remaining cows were too old to conceive, the state had immediately done two things: penned up the few remaining members of the species and put an admission on their viewing, and devised a nationwide lottery to select the persons who would be allowed to hunt—and take the head and hide of—the last American buffalo.

Both moves proved enormously successful. The Last Remaining Buffalo concession, let by the state to one of its own departments, the Bureau of Parks, was open nine months of the year. Managed by park rangers, it operated under very low overhead and was the most profitable tourist attraction in the state. All around the corral where the buffalo were exhibited, there were coin-operated machines where for a quarter visitors could purchase cups of processed food pellets to toss into the corral for the buffalo to eat. Like peanuts to caged monkeys. Except that the buffalo refused to do tricks. Despite considerable effort in the beginning, including the use of a whip, the buffalo had remained stoic and refused to be trained. Finally, the park rangers had to resign themselves to simply leading their charges into the corral and letting them stand there while small children pelted them with synthetic food. The attraction, nevertheless, was popular.

As profitable as the concession was, however, its earnings were modest compared to the proceeds of the lottery. In a scheme devised by one of the General Accounting Office's young financial wizards, two million numbered tickets had been sold throughout the state and through the mail nationally, for five dollars a chance. The ticket supply was exhausted within a month, and the state had made a quick ten million dollars. Even people who had no interest whatever in hunting bought a ticket for investment speculation. Even before the drawing, advertisements had been run by people offering to buy a winning ticket from anyone whose number was picked.

The drawing, wherein three winners were selected, was by the use of a single, predesignated digit each day from the total shares traded on the New York Stock Exchange. The lucky ticket holders were a piano tuner from Boston, a waiter in Memphis, and a ranch hand in Nevada. The piano tuner sold his ticket for ten thousand dollars to Gregory Kingston, the actor. The waiter sold his for eighty-five hundred to best-selling author Harmon Langford. Lester Ash, the ranch hand, kept his, deciding that the head and hide would be worth far more than the ticket. He was counting on being a better hunter and shot than the actor and author were.

Within two hours of the untimely death of Bruno, the three registered owners of the winning tickets were notified to come claim their prize. Hannah, the last surviving plains buffalo, would be released fifty miles out on the prairie at noon on Friday.

At noon on Saturday, the three lottery winners would be free to hunt her.

By midnight on Thursday, Tank Sherman was ready to go. Hitched to the rear of his Ford pickup truck was a double-stall horse trailer from which he had removed the center divider, creating one large stall.

Parking the rig on the prairie some one hundred yards behind the concession corral, he and Delia slipped through the quiet night to the barn, snipped the padlock with bolt cutters, and led Hannah out. The old buffalo cow was as docile as a rabbit and made no noise whatever as Delia fed her a handful of fresh meadow grass and Tank slipped a braided halter over her head.

After walking the buffalo aboard the trailer and quietly closing her in, Tank handed Delia an envelope. "Here's the deed to the cabin and lot. And the passbook to your ma's savings account. She had six hundred and forty dollars saved when she died; it was supposed to be yours when you were twenty-one. Oh, and the title to the pickup is there, too, just in case. Guess that's about all."

Delia got a paper bag and thermos jug from her Jeep. "Sandwiches," she said. "And coffee. With, uh—"

"Yeah." He put the bag and jug on the seat of the pickup and sniffed once as if he might be catching cold. But he wasn't catching cold. "Listen, take care of yourself, kid," he said brusquely, and started to get into the truck. Then he turned back. "Look, I know I ain't never won no Father-of-the-Year prize and I never gave you noplace to live but that cabin and I never sent you to college or nothing, but those things don't have nothing to do with caring. You understand?"

"Sure," Delia said. She shrugged. "After all, you did teach me when to fold in poker. And how to change a flat. And how to get a squirrel to eat out of my hand. Lots of girls never learn those things." She had to struggle to control her voice. She was not able to control her tears. But she knew that Tank couldn't see the tears in the darkness.

"Okay," he said. "I'll be hitting the road then."

He eased the door of the pickup shut, quietly started the engine, and slowly pulled away without headlights.

Behind him, Delia waved in the darkness and said, "Bye—Daddy."

When he reached the highway, turned on his headlights, and increased speed, Tank thought: *Okay, Rose, this is for you, honey.*

Rose was Tank's dead wife, the woman who had always wanted him to do something important. Her Shoshone name was Primrose, given to her by her father because she had been born on a day in early July when the evening primrose had just blossomed. Later, when she moved into town and took up the ways of the white woman, she shortened it to Rose.

Tank always remembered Rose as being beautiful, but she was not; she was not even pretty. Her face was very plain, her eyes set too close together, her nose too long, and one cheek was pitted with pockmarks. Only her hair, lustrous as polished onyx, could truly be called beautiful. But Tank saw so much more of her than was outside. He saw her hopes and dreams, her pride, her nakedness when they made love, her secret joys. He saw everything about her, and it was all of those things combined which made her beautiful to him.

The first time she had shown him the buffalo was three months after she had taken him to live with her, after she had nursed him back to health from the beating he had taken. They got up early one morning on Rose's day off from the sugar-beet processing plant, and in her old Jeep they drove thirty miles out onto the raw prairie. There, on an isolated meadow, was a small buffalo herd: three bulls, a cow, and six calves. They were the beginning of the last migration, when the ocean of tourists had started driving them north and west from the Black Hills.

"See how noble they look," Rose had said. "See the dignity with which they stand and observe." Her eyes had become water and she had added, "They are watching their world come to an end."

Once, Rose explained to him, there had been sixty *million* plains buffalo. Their presence on the Northern Plains had been the greatest recorded aggregation of large land animals ever known to man. To the red man of the prairie, the vast herds had been the mainstay of his economy. That single species provided food, clothing, shelter, and medicine for an entire race—the only time in history that such a natural balance between man and beast had ever been achieved.

"Then, of course, the whites came," Rose said. "At first, they killed the buffalo for meat and hides, as our people did, and that was acceptable because the herds were many. Later they killed them only for hides, leaving the carcasses to rot in the sun. Even that act, although it was without honor, could have been tolerated. But then they began killing them for what they called 'sport.' Fun. Recreation.

"They killed them first by the tens of thousands. The butcher Cody, whom they called 'Buffalo Bill,' personally recorded more than forty-two-thousand kills in one seventeen-month period. Soon they were being slaughtered with total wantonness, by the hundreds of thousands. Today there are only a few hundred left. Most of them are in the Black Hills. But they're slowly migrating back up here again."

"Why?" Tank asked, fascinated.

"They know the end is nearing for them. A species can tell when their breed is running out. Each year they see fewer and fewer calves, the herds become smaller and smaller. So they look for a place to end their line. They look for a grassy meadow unspoiled by humans. A place to lie down and die with dignity."

For all the years Tank Sherman knew and lived with the Shoshone woman Rose, she had loved the great buffalo and mourned its diminishing number. As much as Tank missed her in death, he was glad that she had not lived to see Bruno and Hannah, the last two of the breed, penned up and put on display—or known about the lottery for the privilege of hunting the survivor.

So this is for you, honey, he thought as he headed southeast with Hannah in the horse trailer. He would have about five hours head start. Possibly two hundred fifty miles. Maybe it would be enough.

Maybe not.

Two hours after dawn, a tall, very handsome man, livid with anger, was stalking back and forth in the empty concession corral.

"What the hell do you mean, *missing?* How can something as large as a buffalo be *missing?*" His name was Gregory Kingston. An Academy Award-winning actor, he was not acting now; he was truly incensed.

"The state guaranteed this hunt," said a second man. Smaller, plumper, not as handsome but with a good deal more bearing, this was Harmon Langford, internationally known bestselling author. Like Kingston, he was dressed in expensive hunting garb, carrying a fine, hand-tooled, engraved, foreign-made rifle. "Exactly who's in charge here?" he quietly demanded.

A third man, Lester Ash, the ranch hand from Nevada, stood back a step, not speaking, but observing everything. He wore hardy working clothes: denim, twill, roughout leather.

"Gentlemen," a Bureau of Mines spokesman pleaded, "please believe me, we're trying to get to the bottom of this as quickly as we can. All we know right now is that some person or persons apparently abducted Hannah sometime during the night. The highway patrol has been notified and a statewide search is getting underway at this very moment—"

"Why in hell would anyone want to abduct a *buffalo?*" Kingston inquired loudly of the world at large, throwing his arms up in bewilderment. Now he *was* acting.

"Oh, come, Kingston," said Harmon Langford, "we're not talking about *a* buffalo, we're talking about *this* buffalo. Unlike ourselves, there *are* those"—and here he glanced at Lester Ash—"who are interested in this animal not for sport but for profit." Lester Ash grinned but remained silent. Langford continued, "At any rate, we cannot waste time on *why*—we must concentrate on *where*. *Where* is our great, hairy prize? And how do we get to it?"

The Bureau of Parks man said, "We should be hearing from the highway patrol any time now. Every road in the state is covered."

"What do we do now?" asked Gregory Kingston, directing the question at Langford.

"We must be prepared to get to the animal as quickly as possible after it's located," the author declared. "Before some outsider decides to take an illegal shot at it. This part of the country is crawling with would-be cowboys. Pickup trucks, rifle racks in the back window, old faded Levis—that sort of thing. I'm sure there are a few of them who would like to be remembered as the man who gunned down the last buffalo."

"Like you, you mean?" Lester Ash said, speaking for the first time.

A smirk settled on Langford's lips. "Yes," he acknowledged. Adding, "And you." They locked eyes in a moment of mutual understanding and then Langford said, "What we need, of course, is fast, flexible transportation." He turned to the Parks man. "How far is the nearest helicopter service?"

"Fifty miles."

"I suggest we start at once. If we have a helicopter at our

disposal by the time the buffalo is located, we can hurry there at once. I presume the state would have no objection to that?"

The Parks man shrugged. "No so long as all three of you get an equal start. And don't shoot it from the air."

"Of course not. We aren't barbarians, after all." He looked at Kingston and Lester Ash. "Are we agreed?"

"Agreed," said the actor.

"Let's go," said Ash.

Three hours earlier, Tank had parked the pickup and trailer in a stand of elm and gone on foot deeper into the trees where Otter had his cabin. It had still been dark—the eerie void before dawn. He knocked softly at Otter's door.

"Who disturbs this weak old man at such an hour?" a voice asked from within. "Is it someone evil, come to take advantage of my helplessness?"

"Otter, it's Sherman," said Tank. "Your daughter's man before she passed.

"What is it you want?" asked Otter. "I am destitute and can offer you nothing. I have no money or other valuables. I barely exist from day to day. Why have you come to me?"

"For your wisdom, Otter. For your words."

"Perhaps I can give you that, although I am usually so weak from hunger that each breath could well be my last. How many others have you brought with you?"

Tank smiled in the darkness. "I am alone, Otter." Maybe now the old scoundrel would stop acting.

"You may enter," Otter said. "There are candles by the door."

Inside the front door, Tank lighted a candle that illuminated patches of an incredibly dirty and impoverished room. In one corner, an ancient cot with torn sagging mattress; in another, a rusted iron sink filled with dirty pots and pans; in a third, an old chifforobe with a broken door hanging loose to reveal a few articles of ragged clothing. Everywhere in between there was dirt, grime, clutter.

Tank didn't pause in the room. He lit his way directly to a door which led to a second room, and in that room he found Otter sitting up in a king-size bed, a cigar in his mouth, a bot-

tle of whiskey at his side. As Tank closed the door behind
him, the old Indian uncocked a double-barrel shotgun on the
bed beside him and put it on the floor. "How are you, Soft
Face?" he asked. The first time he had seen Tank, the young
fighter's face had been beaten to pulp. Otter had called him
"Soft Face" ever since.

"I'm okay," Tank said. "You look the same."

The old Indian shrugged. "There is no reason for something
perfect to change."

Tank grinned and glanced around the room. It was a self-
contained little world, holding everything Otter needed or
wanted for his personal comfort. Portable air-conditioner,
color television, microwave oven, upright freezer, power gen-
erator, small bathroom in one corner, indoor hot tub and
jacuzzi in another. "How's the bootlegging business?" Tank
asked.

"My customers are loyal. I make ends meet." Otter got out
of bed and put a Hopi blanket around his shoulders. "Is my
granddaughter still dealing cards in the white man's game?"

"Yes."

"Does she cheat them when the opportunity presents itself?"

"Yes, if they are tourists."

Otter nodded in approval. "That is good. Even a half-Indian
should cheat the whites whenever possible." At a two-burner
hotplate, Otter set water to boil. "Sit here at the table," he said,
"and tell me your problem."

Tank explained to the old Indian what he had done, and
why. When he got to the part about Rose and her love for the
buffalo, Otter's eyes became misty. When Tank stopped talking, Otter rose, poured coffee and brandy for them, and
brought it to the table. "How can I help you?" he asked.

"I need a safe place to put the old buffalo. Someplace where
she can live out her days in peace without fear of being hunted
and shot. Someplace where she will be able to die quietly, like
your daughter Primrose would want her to die."

Otter sipped his coffee and pondered the problem. Several
times he shook his head, as if first considering, then dismiss-
ing, a possibility. Finally he tapped a forefinger on the table

and said, "Do you remember the place where Ditch Creek runs beside Bear Mountain?"

"In the Black Hills?" said Tank. "Where you used to take us on picnics when Delia was a little girl?"

"That's the place. There's a grassy meadow far above Ditch Creek that belongs to the few remaining people of the Deerfield tribe. It's within the Black Hills National Park, but the federal government deeded it to the Deerfields because there was no road into it and they must have figured the tourists wouldn't be able to get to it anyway. The Deerfield use it for religious ceremonies—it's sacred ground to them. The buffalo would be protected once it got there. But there are only dirt paths leading up to the meadow. I don't know if the buffalo could climb it or not."

"How high is it?" Tank asked.

"About seven thousand feet. There's a gravel road to about six thousand, but the rest of the way would be on footpaths. It would have been better if you'd stolen a mountain goat—you never were very smart, Soft Face."

"Can you draw me a map?" Tank asked.

"Of course. I am a man of many talents."

Otter got paper and pencil and from memory sketched a map and gave it to Tank. It was daylight now and the two of them walked out to the horse trailer.

Tank backed Hannah out to exercise and feed her.

"She's a fine old buffalo," Otter observed. "Only your people would think of shooting her."

"Just because they're the same color doesn't mean they're my people," Tank replied.

Tank tethered the buffalo to a tree and returned to the cabin with Otter. The old Indian cooked breakfast and they ate together. Then it was time for Tank to leave. Otter walked back to the rig and helped him load Hannah. After Tank got in and started the truck, Otter put a hand on the door.

"In each man's life, there is a plateau," he said. "Every man reaches that plateau. He may be there for a day or a year, or only for a moment. But his time there is the meaning of his life. It is the reason the Great One put him here on earth. I think, Soft Face, that your plateau might be that grassy meadow above Ditch Creek." He touched Tank's shoulder. "Go with the wind, son."

Tank swallowed dryly, nodded, and drove off.

The helicopter was flying a checkerboard search pattern two hundred miles from where the buffalo had been stolen. Harmon Langford sat next to the pilot. Gregory Kingston and Lester Ash occupied jumpseats behind them. All three men scanned the ground below with binoculars.

"This is maddening," Kingston muttered. He tapped Langford on the shoulder. "Tell me again!" he yelled through the noise of the rotor. "Why are we looking in this direction?"

The author yelled back, "The highway patrol reported that a pickup truck pulling a horse trailer filled up with gas in Dayton at four o'clock this morning! The station attendant said the animal in the trailer had a blanket over it and the man driving the truck said it was a rodeo bull! But he thinks it was our buffalo! They were headed toward Gillette! We're searching the area south of Gillette!"

The actor shrugged, as if it were all totally meaningless to him. Lester Ash leaned close to his ear and said, "Highway Patrol thinks he might be headed toward Thunder Basin! That's a big grassland area! Be a perfect place to set a buffalo loose!"

"I see!" Kingston said, smiling. "Now *that* makes sense!" He patted Ash fondly on the knee. Ash drew back suspiciously.

The helicopter continued to checkerboard, its pilot crossing out squares on a plot map on the console. They flew well into the grasslands, twenty miles deep, and began a random searching pattern, following shadows, wind movement, wild game—anything that attracted their attention. But they didn't find what they were looking for.

After an hour, the pilot advised Langford, "We'll have to land for fuel soon."

No sooner had he spoken, they received a radio message from the Parks man back at the concession. "The trailer has been sighted by a Civil Air Patrol scout plane. It's on Route 16, south of Osage, heading toward the Black Hills. It's sure to make it across the state line, so we're requesting the South Dakota state police to set up roadblocks. I'll keep you advised."

"How far is Osage?" Langford asked the pilot.

"Fifty miles, give or take."

"Can we make it?"

"Yessir, but that'll be the limit. We'll have to refuel in Osage."

"Go," Harmon Langford ordered.

Tank had his CB tuned to the law-enforcement band, so he heard the South Dakota state police order go out for roadblocks. They were being set up in Custer, Four Corners, and at the junction of Routes 85 and 16. Pulling onto the shoulder of the road, Tank shifted to neutral and unfolded a map he'd picked up at a service station near Sundance, where Otter lived. When he'd stopped at the station, the tarp flaps on the trailer had been down so no one could see inside. He was sure it hadn't been the station attendant who put the law on him. Probably that low-flying two-seater that had come in over him outside Osage.

Studying the map, Tank saw that the locations selected for the roadblocks gave him considerably more leeway than he had expected. Apparently they thought he was going to try to drive well into the Black Hills. He wasn't. He needed to penetrate them only a few miles before reaching a secondary road that ran north and then east to Ditch Creek. Smiling, he saw that he would reach all three roadblocks. Getting out of the truck for a moment, he lifted one of the trailer flaps and reached in to pat Hannah's thick, hairy cape.

"We're going to beat the sons of bitches, old girl," he said happily.

It hadn't occurred to him that they might use a helicopter.

At Osage, Harmon Langford conferred by a telephone with the authorities responsible for the roadblock. "Of course, I very much appreciate your help in containing this man, Captain, and I assure you that when I write about this incident, you and your men will be prominently featured. Now if you'd just be good enough to keep your forces in place and let my associates and me handle it from here, I think justice will be properly served. We really don't consider this a criminal matter. It's more mischief than anything else—a nuisance, but we can handle it."

Then he talked with the pilot of the scout plane. "Are you keeping him in sight?"

"Yes, Mr. Langford. He's moving up a secondary road toward a place called Ditch Creek."

"Fine. Keep circling and don't lose him. We'll be airborne again in a few minutes and should be there shortly. Of course, I'll expect to see you after this is all over, for photographs and such. Over and out."

As Langford turned to face them, Kingston and Lester Ash saw a look of gleeful triumph on his face. Almost an evil look.

"In a very short while, gentlemen," he said, "we should be in position to take our buffalo back. I trust both of you are prepared to deal with this abductor if he resists us?"

Kingston frowned. "What do you mean?"

Langford did not answer. Instead, he picked up his rifle and jacked a round into the chamber.

Watching him, Lester Ash smiled.

Turning off the secondary road into the inclining gravel road, Tank was aware that the patrol plane was following him. But he wasn't overly concerned. The two men in the light plane couldn't get to him. There was noplace in the surrounding hills they could land. All they could do was radio his position and he was too close to his goal now for that to matter. He knew where the roadblocks were—no one from there could catch up with him. Only one obstacle remained in his way: the thousand feet of footpath from the end of the gravel road up to the meadow.

Frowning, he wondered if old Hannah was going to be able to make it. A lot would depend on how steep the trail was and what kind of footing it offered. Good dirt footing was what he hoped for—Hannah's freshly trimmed hooves would slide too much on rock.

At the end of the gravel road, Tank drove the rig as far into the trees as he could. Part of the trailer still stuck out and he knew it could be seen from the air. No matter, he thought, they can't catch us now.

"Come on, old girl," he said as he backed Hannah out of the trailer and rubbed her neck. Studying the terrain above them, he selected the least steep path he could find and gently pulled Hannah onto it. Moving about four feet ahead of her, he drew the halter rope tight and urged her forward. She stepped nimbly up the trail and followed him without resistance.

This might be easier than I thought, Tank told himself hopefully.

The helicopter rendezvoused with the scout plane an hour after Tank and Hannah began their climb.

"Where are they?" Langford asked the air-patrol pilot on the radio.

"In those trees on the side of the mountain, sir. You can't see them right now because of the overgrowth. They're probably about halfway up to that grassy meadow on the plateau there."

Langford praised the two men in the plane for exemplary work, dismissed them, and turned to the helicopter pilot. "Set down on that grassy meadow," he ordered.

"I can't do that, sir," said that pilot, who was half Nez Perce. "That's sacred land belonging to the Deerfield tribe. Outsiders aren't permitted there."

Langford shifted the barrel of his rifle until it pointed toward the pilot. "I really do want you to land," he said pointedly.

The Nez Perce smiled. "I'd be careful with that rifle if I were you, sir. Unless you or your friends know how to fly one of these babies. They go down mighty fast."

Pursing his lips, Langford shifted the barrel back. He reached into his pocket, extracted a roll of currency, and peeled off five one-hundred-dollar bills. "If you could just hover a few feet from the ground. Long enough for us to drop off."

"That," the pilot said, taking the money, "I can do."

The last few hundred feet were the worst for both the man and the buffalo. The trail, after an easy beginning, had become narrow, steep, rutted, and treacherous. Three times, Hannah's hooves slipped on loose rocks or concealed roots and she went sliding back fifteen or twenty feet, dragging Tank with her. Each time, she rolled over onto her side and mooed anxiously as dirt from above displaced and shifted down to half bury her. Each time, Tank had to stroke and soothe her, help her dig out and regain her balance and patiently urge her forward again.

Twice Tank himself slipped badly, the leather of his old boots reacting just as Hannah's hooves did to the hostile ground under them. The first time he fell, his left foot came out from under him and he pitched onto both knees, puncturing one trouser leg on a sharp rock and cutting his knee badly enough to bleed. The second time, he lost his balance completely and went plunging downhill, sliding helplessly past Hannah, his face, shirt, and boots catching the avalanche of loose dirt that followed him. He had the presence of mind to let go of the halter rope, and didn't upset Hannah with his spill, but he slid all of forty feet. When he straightened himself, he was filthy with dirt stuck to his sweaty clothes and body and his face and hands showed nicks and cuts seeping blood through the dirt. Cursing mightily, Tank clawed his way back up to where Hannah, watching him curiously, waited with infinite patience.

Late in the climb, perhaps two hundred feet from the plateau, Tank thought he heard the roar of a motor. It was hard to tell with the thick treetops insulating the ground from noise and the constant wind whipping about now that they were so high. Maybe it was that light plane coming in low to search the meadow. If so, he thought craftily, they would find nothing there.

We're beating them, Rose—Hannah and me. And it's important that we beat them. Important that we make that plateau.

They kept climbing, the man and the buffalo, struggling against the total environment around them—the height aloof above them, the ground resistant under them, the air thin and selfish, the dirt and dust, the rocks and roots. Blood and sweat burned their eyes, both of them, for Hannah now had cuts on her old face as well. Foam coated her lips, saliva and tears wet the man's cheeks.

They climbed until their muscles came close to locking, their lungs close to bursting, their hearts close to breaking. With no resource left but blind courage, they climbed.

Finally, they made it to the top and together crawled onto the edge of the grassy meadow.

The three hunters were waiting there for them.

Only when he saw the hunters did Tank Sherman realize that the motor roar he heard had not been the scout plane but a helicopter. As he and the buffalo struggled together to drag their bodies over the lip of the plateau, both had fallen onto their knees, Tank pitching forward so that he was on all fours, Hannah with her front legs bent, great head down. Both were panting, trying to suck enough oxygen out of the thin air to cool lungs that felt as if they had been singed. For one brief instant, as they knelt side by side. Tank's shoulder brushing Hannah's neck, both their heads hung, as if man and beast were one.

Then Tank looked up and saw the hunters. They stood in a row, the sun reflecting on their rifles.

"No," he said softly, shaking his head. "No," a little louder as he got to his feet. "No!" he yelled as he walked toward them.

Harmon Langford, standing in the middle, said, "Stop where you are—come any closer and we'll shoot!"

Eyes fixed like a madman, jaw clenched like a vise, his big fists closed, Tank stalked toward them. "No!" he kept shouting. "No! No! No!"

"You've been warned!" snapped Langford.

Tank kept coming.

"All right, shoot him!" Langford ordered, shouldering his own rifle and aiming.

No shots were fired. Langford lowered his rifle and looked frantically from Kingston to Lester Ash. "Shoot! Why don't you shoot?"

"Why don't you?" Lester Ash asked evenly.

Langford didn't have time to reply. Tank reached him, snatched the rifle from his hands, and hurled it away. Then he drove a crushing right fist into Langford's face, smashing his nose and lips, sending him reeling back in shock.

As Langford fell, Tank turned to Gregory Kingston. "Now just a minute," the actor pleaded. "I had no intention of shooting you—" He threw down the rifle as evidence of his sincerity, but that didn't deter Tank. The old fighter dug a solid right fist deep into Kingston's midsection and the actor folded up like a suitcase, the color draining from his face, his eyes bulging. Dropping to his knees, he pitched forward onto his face, the juicy meadow grass staining it green.

When Tank looked for the third man, he found that Lester Ash, experienced hunter that he was, had flanked his adversary and moved around behind him. It was now Tank standing on the meadow, Lester Ash facing him with his back to the sun.

"We can do it the easy way or the hard way, bud," said Lester. "Either way, that buffalo's mine."

Tank shook his head. "No." He moved toward Ash.

"I ain't no loud-mouthed writer or sissy actor, bud," the Nevadan said. "Mess with me and I'll put you in the hospital. That buff is *mine!*"

"No." Tank kept coming.

"Please yourself," Lester said disgustedly. He snapped the rifle to his shoulder and fired.

The round ripped all the way through the fleshy part of Tank's left thigh and knocked him off his feet. Instincts two decades old still lived in his mind, and as if someone were counting ten over him Tank rolled over and got back up. Clutching his thigh, he limped toward Ash.

"You're a damned fool, bud," said Lester Ash. He fired again.

The second slug tore a hole in Tank's right thigh and he was again spun to the ground. He moaned aloud, involuntarily, and sat up, one hand on each wound. Pain seared his body, hot and relentless, and he began to choke, cough, and cry. I'm done for, he thought.

Then at his feet he saw something white and yellow. Pawing the tears from his eyes, he managed to focus. It was a clump of wildflowers—white petals with yellow nectarines. Primroses.

Tank dragged himself up one last time. He started forward again, weaving and faltering like a drunk man. His eyes fixed on Lester Ash and held.

"Okay, bud," said Lester, "now you lose a kneecap—"

Before Lester could fire, Hannah charged. Massive head down, hooves almost soundless on the thick meadow grass, she was upon Lester Ash before he realized it. Catching him from the left side, her broad forehead drove into his chest, crushing his left rib cage, collapsing the lung beneath it. With his body half bent over her face, Hannah propelled him to the edge of the plateau and hurled him over the side.

Lester Ash screamed as his body ricocheted off the first three trees, then was silent for the rest of the way down.

The Deerfield tribe marshal and his deputy, who rode up to the meadow on horseback at the first sound of gunfire, secured the area and arranged for Harmon Langford and Gregory Kingston to be escorted down to the reservation boundary. They were released with a stern warning never to violate Deerfield land again. Some men with a rescue stretcher retrieved Lester Ash's body. His death was officially attributed to an accidental fall from the plateau.

A Deerfield medicine man named Alzada, who resided in a lodge back in the trees next to the meadow, was consulted by the marshal as to the disposition of the buffalo.

"If the Great One put the buffalo here," Alzada decreed, "then the buffalo must be sacred. It shall be allowed to graze on the sacred meadow until the Great One summons it back."

The marshal looked over at the edge of the meadow where Tank sat under a tree, exhausted and bleeding. "What about the man?"

"What man?" said Alzada. "I see no man. I see only a sacred buffalo, grazing contentedly. If you see something else, perhaps it is a spirit.

The marshal shook his head. "If Alzada sees nothing, then I see nothing. Only Alzada can see spirits."

The marshal and his deputy rode back down the mountain.

When they were gone, the medicine man went over and helped Tank into the trees to his lodge.

DAY OF THE TIGER

JACK WEBB

The third shot fired by Officer Shelby struck Dandy Fornos in the calf of his left leg. It was a slight wound, cutting through the edge of the flesh, slashing twice through the cheap wool of his charcoal slacks, but it put the fear of the devil in his heart and wings on his heels. He did not drop the briefcase which was all that was left of the shambles behind him: the car with its engine block smashed by a .357 Magnum slug; Ronnie and Joe, dead; the cop crumpled behind the wheel of the black and white sedan, and the other on his stomach in the road, shooting, shooting.

Away to the right was a line of thick shrubs along a high steel mesh fence. Dandy turned and fled toward them.

Shirley Duffy braked her car hard and fast and pressed the horn. What was the crazy fool doing, rushing blindly across this side street, sport coat flying, clutching that silly briefcase with both hands?

North from the way she was driving, more sirens than before were wailing. She was glad she had come into the park over the bridge from the south. She was in no mood to be stopped by a fire or an accident, however grim it might be.

She parked the small sport coupe competently a little way from the entrance of the zoo. What a foolish place to meet, but it was safe. Tom was clever about such things, almost too clever.

Her long legs were elegant as they reached from the edge of the seat to the pavement. Her blue silk suit was freshly pressed, and her soft brown hair shone in the sunlight. She was quite young, pretty, and in love. It showed in the way she walked and in the proud way she carried her shoulders as she hastened toward a destiny where all birds sang.

At the turnstile to the zoological gardens, she had to wait while the man ahead of her received his change.

He was a slim individual, neither much older nor much taller than she. His thin, blond hair was sparse at the temples, and his gray flannel, although it had been a good suit once, was shabby now, not so much with wear but as though he no longer cared about his personal appearance—like his shoes, good leather, well shaped, but desperately needing a polish.

Tom would never become like that, she thought. Vaguely, Shirley felt a little sorry for the unhappy young man. But this was no day for that! This was a day for casting away all regrets, all fears . . .

Not so for Allen Trask. He hurried away from the pretty girl behind him at the turnstile, for there had been something in the tilt of her chin, the directness of her brown eyes, that had reminded him of Anne—not much, but enough. Now Anne was dead, and he had killed her as surely as though he had held a knife, taken a gun . . .

He did not pause at the reptile house, which came first along the road to the exhibits. Snakes were dreadful things, death in a coil, death in a shady corner, and he had had enough of death.

Then, coming to the zoo, there had been the siren, and now there were more, running closer, and it was all beginning again—the dread cry that had been there in the night, the first sound he had heard after smashing through the guard rail; seeing the lights askew where the car had crashed, hearing the scream, the terrible cry of the sirens coming, focusing on the distorted ring of faces about him, finding awful words to ask and no one to tell him of Anne, of Anne who had been on the seat beside him . . .

At a cage of macaws, he paused. With their wise, sober eyes, they regarded him from clown faces. Each bird was clothed in bright feathers, blue and yellow, red and green; glorious birds. One, with a bright yellow breast and long banners of blue for wings, hooked its way down the tall side of steel

mesh until it hung opposite him. "Pretty Polly," it rasped at
Allen Trask.

"Pretty Polly," Allen said bleakly.

The girl went by, her tall heels clicking. The gaudy parrots
watched the girl.

"Pretty Polly," Allen repeated.

The blue and yellow macaw grumbled.

Through the glass door marked DIRECTOR, John Krueger
saw the boy with the briefcase fumble for the price of admission, enter the zoo, and hurry out of sight down the road toward the reptile house. It was a warm day, but not so warm
that beads of perspiration should stand out on the boy's forehead, and why did he hurry so much with such a difficult
limp? Krueger's eyes crinkled thoughtfully. He would not
admit to his premonitions, yet the very business he was in depended upon them. Take those two cocky sailors last week—
something about the way they had laughed. They had bothered
him so much he had followed them later, and found them heat-
ing pennies with a cigarette lighter to toss into a cageful of in-
quisitive monkeys.

The phone rang on his desk. He lifted it and listened. "Sheba's begun," Pete told him. His tone was excited. "Doc Chapman thought you would want to come."

"You bet," Krueger said to the cat keeper. "Take care of
things till I get there."

At the door to his office, Krueger paused to speak to the girl
at the switchboard. "I'm going to be busy, Marge. The tiger's
cubs are coming."

"Yes, Mr. Krueger."

He went out the door and climbed into his car. Last year,
they had lost Sheba's litter. This time . . . He started the car
and swung it around onto the road. There was a spot of color,
and another, and another, shining dark in the sunlight against
the pavement top. Krueger slowed and stared at the road.
Blood! Not much, but certainly blood. The young man with
the limp? He recalled hearing sirens.

He thought of phoning the police, but rejected the idea. He
wanted no troop of policemen tramping about the park, not

until Sheba's cubbing was over. The slightest unnatural movement, sudden sound, unknown voice could wreck everything.

If the boy *were* a fugitive, he would remain quiet, unobtrusive. Krueger frowned and drove on. Perhaps he was letting his mind run away, but in a zoo you become so conscious of a spot or two of blood, of the trouble it could mean inside a cage, that you never see it without translating those blots into a dangerous possibility.

The limping young man was not in sight as he drove down the road into the canyon.

The small, open amphitheater where the trained seals performed each afternoon was empty. Slowly, painfully, Dandy Fornos made his way among the tiers of seats until he was out of sight from the rim of the bowl. There he sat upon a step, stretching his left leg stiffly before him. The pain blossomed up from the calf and shook his whole body. Every nerve was still taut with the near thing, the real. Not yet twenty, slight of build and dark, he would have been handsome except for his eyes which were like those of the lean gray wolf in the canyon below.

He set the briefcase down beside him. What a lousy price for Ronny and Joe, for the wrecked car and the dead cop; for the hurt pulsing through him only a slow pace behind the beat of his heart.

Dandy found his handkerchief and carefully pulled up his left trouser leg. He thought about the car which had nearly run him down, of its being parked before the zoo. *If she were here!*

A sudden, hard thump hit the rail at the top of the amphitheater behind his back. Dandy swung around, his hand sliding under his coat.

The big blue peacock settled on the rail, arched its neck, tilted its head from one side to the other, and examined him with beady eyes before it stretched a striped wing to peck unconcernedly at a loose feather.

Dandy Fornos swore. He would have to get out of this damned fishbowl.

                    *   *   *

Shirley Duffy glanced at her watch. It was almost a quarter till eleven. Tom had said ten. So often she had had to wait for Tom in these hidden places, but not after today. This was to be the end of that sort of thing. Tom had promised.

Down the line, the shabby young man who had preceded her into the zoo was leaning against the rail and smiling. Something in that particular monkey cage was amusing him. She was glad he was happy even for a moment. He had looked so beaten, so nondescript. Now that he was smiling, he was almost attractive. Of course, he could not be handsome, not with his scalp shining through his thinning hair. Tom had a wonderful head of hair, dark, just beginning to fleck with gray, perfectly groomed. Tom was distinguished. Women looked at Tom Connors and envied her. Men liked him. Tom should have been in the diplomatic corps, but he had been waiting for her—in spite of the mistake of his marriage. Shirley sighed and it was almost like the pleasure of his touch.

The man in the shabby flannels laughed aloud. It was so unexpected that Shirley strolled down the line of cages to see what had caused his good humor. The sign on the cage front read:

DIANA MONKEY
(Cercopithecus diana roloway)
West Africa

Behind the steel mesh, a dark, triangular-faced monkey with a black Vandyke and a snowy chest was meticulously examining a scrawny baby. The little old man looked so much like a proud grandfather inspecting his first grandson that Shirley smiled, too. A female monkey beside the pair chattered nervously while three others watched in attitudes of bright expectancy.

"Mama's worried about Gramp," Shirley said.

When she spoke, the man turned. "Yes," he said, "isn't she?" Most of the good humor fled his face.

"I'm sorry," Shirley said tartly, "I didn't mean to intrude."

"Please, you didn't. Believe me . . ."

"Ah, there you are."

They both turned and Shirley exclaimed, "Tom!" She ran to the handsome, middle-aged man, her hands extended.

Allen Trask returned to the cage full of Diana monkeys. There were no complications in monkeys, only a full-of-lifeness, only an entertainment.

Down in the canyon, Sheba was moaning; it was low and full-bodied and almost human. Crouched in a corner behind the tall rear wall of the cat grotto, almost out of sight, Krueger, Pete the keeper, and Dr. Chapman the veterinarian watched and listened. Krueger had parked his car and walked down to join the two men.

Gently, almost secure in her time of pain, the tigress began to work at the tenuous sheath surrounding the first of her newborns.

"Sheba," Pete called softly, "Sheba, Sheba-girl." It was as though there were a communion between the keeper and the cat. Dr. Chapman raised a warning finger. Then he saw that the cat had heard and was not afraid. There was nothing about this in all the books he had ever read on veterinary medicine—except where house pets were concerned, of course—but this was a tiger, savage, neurotic, and unpredictable.

"Sheba," the stocky keeper chanted, "Sheba, Sheba," and the miracle in the cave went on.

It went on without Sultan, for the big male Amurian tiger was in a strange place. Yesterday morning, after a full day of fasting, he had been trapped in a carrying cage pushed against the rear door of the grotto where he had spent five years with Sheba, and moved to a circus wagon which stood in the "off limits" area on the side of the hill above.

For more than a day and a night now, he had carried his ears flat against the golden orange velvet of his mammoth skull, his tail twitching at the slightest sound, and the snarl in his throat was a constant anger. All the tameness of his captivity was gone, all the security, as he paced the narrow cage, feeling strength in the coil of muscles beneath the black and gold of his shoulders.

It was an old cage on wheels, a cage that had rattled and rumbled across the country a hundred times and more. With

plumed horses before it, it had paraded the streets from Portland, Oregon, to Portland, Maine, from 'Frisco to St. Augus-
tine. A great hulk of teak and iron and oak, of peeling gilt and
shining memories, Krueger had bought it for the zoo when a
shoestring circus had folded in town. No one had thought it
would not hold a tiger.

"Strongest cage I ever seen," Pete had said. Nor had anyone
doubted or even taken the time to look closely at all the bolts
and nuts and hinges.

A peahen came out of the bush before the cage and paused
to peck at a tuft of weed. Behind her, swift and driving, came
a male. When he discovered they were in the open, the peacock halted his plunging run, fanned his tail rigid, and forced
upward the spectacular three-quarter circle of his train, a shim-
mering arch of green and blue. His bulky body quivered, and
the stiff quills of his feathers rattled.

The drab peahen paid him no attention.

Sultan did. Flat on his belly, his eyes shaded to black and
light slits, the tiger felt his muscles grow with tension. The tip
of his tail beat like a metronome.

The peacock continued to strut and shake and bow with
quick, vibrant, excited movements.

Suddenly, the alchemy of his rage and his instincts becom-
ing one overwhelming wave, Sultan charged. He was three
feet off the floor when he hit the heavy bars of the cage door.
The tremendous impact knocked him flat.

The birds fled.

Through the somber furnace of his eyes, Sultan saw the
door at the end of the cage swing open, smashed from the
rusted hinge bolts of almost a century, to dangle by the new
lock and hasp. As softly as a domestic cat going down an alley
in the night, the great Amurian tiger slipped from the cage and
vanished beneath a bloom of white oleanders.

Nor was Sultan the only one who had gone into hiding.

Under the luxuriant leaf-fall of a weeping willow, Dandy
Fornos lay with his head on his briefcase to wait out the inter-
minable hours of daylight. In the seclusion of his green bower,
Dandy had opened the briefcase and counted the contents.

Twenty grand and some odd green. What a hell of a poor haul that would have been to split three ways. Tonight he would cross the wires on some car, some little, unnoticeable car, before one of the big apartments off Twelfth Avenue and head south—not directly to Tijuana, but on a road that angled east from Chula Vista, farther east than the tall, barbed border fence extended. There was a girl in the Midnight Cabaret who would put him up, take care of him. His left leg throbbed steadily.

On the beach beyond the last long droop of willow boughs were a man and a girl—the girl who had been behind the wheel of the coupe that had almost driven him down. He did not worry any more about her. This chick had troubles of her own. Foolish troubles, silly troubles, but they helped pass the time. Dandy cocked his head and listened.

"But I feel like such a fool!" Shirley said. Her voice was cold, and hurt, and trembling a little. "No more than a cheap affair. I'm no more than a tramp! A tramp!"

"Shirley, Shirley." The dapper man with flecks of gray in his hair held her hand and stroked it gently. "Surely you understand it is better to do these things without a scene, without unnecessary noise and confusion. You know how I hate scenes."

She pulled herself together, her hair still shining in the sunlight that filtered through the tall gray trees, her eyes suspiciously puffy as though she had been crying.

"After all," Tom said evenly, "there is my wife, Helen, to be considered."

"Helen," Shirley repeated after him. "Helen!"

For three years it had been Helen. From that very first not-quite-innocent luncheon there always had been Helen, Shirley thought. Once, she had believed, if not me, then some other, some other who might hurt him. From her safe, sacrosanct cubbyhole beside the vice-president's office, she had looked down the line of desks to Accounting, and Tom, so sweet, so vulnerable . . . He did have such hell at home—so many times he had told her.

"Helen," Shirley repeated aloud, breaking the spell of her lost enchantment.

"After all," he said uneasily, "she is my wife."

"I know. I know. I know. I know." She began to cry.

This was the nuts, Dandy Fornos thought, better than TV, better than the movies. What a racket this joe had had. He almost forgot the throb in his leg, the ache that was reaching up through his thigh like a knife.

Allen Trask had not meant to see her again. The zoo was a big place. He had let the girl go to her tryst. Now, coming down the canyon road from the opposite direction, he was running into her again, her with tears on her face, her and that sleek bum. Resolutely, he turned his back and stared into the lion pit:

LION
Panthera leo
Africa

The big lion lolled in the midmorning sun. His shaggy mane was thick and dark and ragged at the edges as though it needed a good brushing. He did not look fierce. In face, Allen Trask smiled, he looked more like the Cowardly Lion of Oz. In spite of the girl, the zoo had been good to Allen. It had taken him back before Anne, before that awful night; it had taken him back to himself.

Only now the girl was here once more, and though he had smiled at the lion, he could feel the tears shining on her cheeks. What good were tears? You should not brood so much, Allen, Dr. Bruce had said. It isn't natural. Then, a month or two ago, Do you mind if I suggest another doctor?

The lion yawned. Allen watched, unseeing.

He had taken the card Dr. Bruce had scribbled and gone up a flight of stairs in the Professional Building, turned right, gone down the long corridor, and stood before the door. Like the signs here in the zoo:

Dr. Anthony B. Connors
Ph.D., M.D.
Psychiatrist

He had not gone through the door. He wasn't insane. It was only that he must pay for the accident. One way or another you paid for everything you did in this life. And he was paying. God knew he was paying—God, and Anne!

Shirley whispered, "You're cheating us, Tom. You're cheating all of us. You, Helen, me . . ."

"Shirley!" The man was rubbing his hands together.

For cripe's sake, Dandy Fornos thought. The pain in his leg made his muscles jerk. Uncomfortably, he rearranged himself, turned his head from the couple on the bench, and gazed into the terrifying black, orange, and white mask of a living tiger.

Allen Trask walked on to the sign that read: AMURIAN TIGERS. No cats were in sight, and he did not notice the group across the way.

On the other side of the empty grotto, Krueger whispered excitedly, "That's her fourth, that should be the lot of them!"

The veterinarian nodded, grinning. Impulsively, the keeper squeezed the elbow of his boss. Krueger smiled. Inside the cave, Sheba began to work on the thin envelope surrounding the furry, squirming weight of her fourth-born.

Sultan knew that he had come home. With that driving, constant instinct which is the birthright of every cat, Sultan had found his way back to the grotto. And now, under the leafy bower that led toward his mate, lay this human being exuding the scent of fear. Sultan bared his fangs and snarled.

Dandy Fornos scrambled backwards, his hand sliding under his coat, the briefcase left behind.

"Tiger!" he screamed. "Tiger!"

He came around the bench running, paying no attention to the ramming pain of every pounding stride. Tom Connors saw the tiger, and ran ahead of the boy, leaving Shirley. She stood before the bench, seeing the soft velvet of black and gold through a tracery of shadows, seeing the great yellow eyes with their bright shining centers as the big cat crept forward. She was unable to move, unable to take a step.

Then a man's body crashed into hers, knocking her down, covering her. She tried to struggle.

"For the love of heaven, be still," he whispered hoarsely.

She could feel the fear consuming his slender body, and beyond the fear, the courage that held him there, the two of them one and together on the other side of a flimsy wooden bench from the creeping tiger.

Sultan sprang, following the runners, pursuing the moving enemy who had come between him and his own.

Dandy Fornos, rocking unevenly on his bad leg, turned his head and saw the tiger coming, one seven-league leap and then another. He knew where the next would be. Instantly, Dandy swung and stood steady, the big automatic bucking as he squeezed the trigger. The last shot was almost in the tiger's throat. They died together, each with the same wild, desperate valor.

Then Allen Trask came to his feet and went down the road to see if there was anything he could do. Tom Connors stood beyond all of them, wiping his brow, while Shirley pulled herself unsteadily onto the bench and watched.

At the first shot, Sheba had risen from her litter. At the second, she had gone snarling into the open air of the grotto beyond her cave. Before the third explosion, the last, Dr. Chapman had pulled the lever that let the steel grate slide down to separate Sheba from her cubs.

It was all over finally. What was left of the boy and the tiger were removed from the canyon, the briefcase was found, the questions asked, Shirley's elegant Tom disappearing before the interrogation. Dr. Chapman and Pete removed the cubs, carrying them all in a wicker basket, incubator babies now.

Left alone, Shirley Duffy and Allen Trask walked up a path shady with trees, each a stranger not so much to each other as to themselves.

"Why did you do it?" she asked.

He shrugged. "It was the only way."

"But you ran toward the tiger." Her brown eyes regarded him soberly.

"You were there. If I could knock you down, if the cat jumped the bench . . ." He let it go.

"The others were running," she said.

"I thought of that," he admitted, "but so was I, and if the cat had to take somebody . . ."

She reached then and touched his hand. "You were willing?"

"It would not have made much difference. For a long time, it wouldn't have made much difference."

Still, she thought, it was for me he did it. "Will you take me home?" she asked.

"I don't have a car."

"I do."

"I haven't driven for a long time," Allen said.

"I can drive."

"No," he said, "you shouldn't."

They turned and retraced their steps toward the entrance to the zoo. As they strolled, Allen began to talk, starting slowly at first, and then letting the words spill like waters loosed from a dam.

Shirley took his hand finally and held it in her own. There was fear there, all his nerves screaming from the fingertips, but beyond that was the courage—and the pent-up longing of a man who had been in the prison of his own soul. Shirley still held his hand as they went out the gate.

Krueger saw them go from the glass pane in his office door. Well, now, he thought. Well, now, and what do you make of that? But he had no time to make anything of it. Zoos are too busy for that sort of thing.

YOUR PENGUIN
OR MINE?

BRUCE SCATES

One a certain night Rona Durant decided to leave her husband. She wouldn't even tell him she was leaving. ("The bastard!") *Freedom!*

On a certain night Jerry Durant decided to leave Rona Durant, his wife. He wouldn't even tell her he was leaving. ("The bitch!") *Freedom!*

On a certain night Eddie Spang decided to practice his profession at a rambling Colonial-style house in the suburbs. *Burglary!*

On a certain night a state-of-the-art blonde coed whose major was cheerleading and whose minor was "Illegal Substances: Their Care and Distribution" decided to stand under a window of the house next door to hers and moan. *Moaning!*

With her perfect hair, her perfect teeth, her perfect perpetually dilated, peerlessly depraved green eyes glowing in the dark, Bobbi Whittier clutched a tennis racket and moaned: "Anyone for tennis?" She whimpered: "Come and play games with me, Jerr." She growled tigerishly: "I want your forehand." She panted: "Yes I said yes I will yes receive your overhead smash!"

Jerry Durant had started giving Bobbi Whittier tennis lessons when she was eleven years old. He had started giving her tennis rackets, jeans, record albums, concert tickets, compact disc players, and the Pill when she was 35–18–34.

"I want your child," Bobbi moaned up at the window. "Or your fur coat, whichever comes first."

Bobbi bounced a can of tennis balls in her right hand. She threw the can of tennis balls through Jerry Durant's bedroom window. Glass tinkled.

"I also want your Porsche, Jerr!"

Blackmail!

In the Durants' living room:

"See-you-in-the-morning," said Jerry Durant, a puffy-faced man of forty-three who pretended to have lustrous jet-black hair, eyebrows, and mustache with the help of Clairol dye. He also pretended to be an honest businessman (*Jerry's* BIG SAVINGS *Appliances*) with the help of deeply and movingly creative bookkeeping which he did himself. (*Two sets*—and they were both honeys.)

"See-you-in-the-morning," said Rona Durant, who was five feet eleven, had a palely dimpled Scandinavian face, wore a pair of flaxen braids, and looked as if she could wrestle professionally under the name of "Heidi the Hun." She was also terribly nearsighted but wouldn't wear her glasses except in bed, where she claimed she needed them to detect certain teeny parts of Jerry's anatomy. (The Durants currently slept in separate bedrooms. They also had zero children and one point five marriages each.)

Jerry looked at Rona and lifted his glass of scotch to her and smiled. *God, how I hate that woman.*

Rona looked at Jerry and narrowed her eyelids to thin slits and smiled back at him. *God, how I hate that man.*

Scratch, scratch, scratch.

Eddie Spang, burglar, twenty-nine years old, crouched in some bushes he hoped to God weren't poison ivy or some bushes crouched on him which he *really* hoped to God weren't poison ivy. But he knew—*knew*—they were poison ivy. To Eddie all bushes that grew outside the safety of the city and

God-made concrete and asphalt were poison ivy. The suburbs
were a *jungle!*

Eddie watched and waited and scratched and carried on a
vigorous inner dialogue:

"What was that?"

"A twig."

"You're sure?"

"It was a twig."

"What was *that?*"

"ANOTHER twig."

"A what?"

"A goddam flying twig!"

"A ——!"

"WHEN ARE THESE PEOPLE GOING TO BED?"

Eddie wished he could see just one mugger. Or even a single run-of-the-mill pervert. So he could feel at home. Something reassuring. *Normal.*

"What was that?"

"A mosquito."

"Ohhhmmyyygoddd!"

In her bedroom (formerly *their* bedroom) Rona Durant telephoned Barry Frisbie, an assistant tennis pro at their country
club. Barry had a great forehand, great hair (blond, curly),
great muscles (everywhere), and only two thoughts in his
head: tennis and sex. Rona had reached the age when she had
only three thoughts in her head: tennis, sex, and money. Barry
wasn't perfect but two out of three wasn't bad.

"Barry? *Rona.* Pick me up in twenty minutes. We're going
south of the border."

"Gee, will I need shots?"

"Smallpox, malaria, the Black Death, and rabies."

She could hear his forehead ripple over the telephone.
"Wow, rabies?"

Rona said, *"Woof, woof."* Then she hung up. Giggling.

Putting on her eyeglasses, Rona picked up her suitcase. Just
simple things she'd need. A few clothes, a *lot* of credit cards.
Her jewelry case. A pair of matched antique silver candle-
sticks that had been in Jerry's family for years and that she

took to remember Jerry's mother by. (She remembered Jerry's mother staring at her and saying to her son: *"So who's your fat friend?"* AT THE WEDDING RECEPTION!)

Also she packed a stuffed toy penguin with a yellow rubber beak that glowed in the dark and whose top-hatted head unscrewed and concealed a secret cavity where she kept a little something that made her head unscrew.

She decided to take a quick shower before Barry arrived.

Pack, pack, pack.

In his bedroom (formerly the guestroom), Jerry Durant packed a suitcase. Bare necessities. A few bottles of scotch. The plaid sports jacket Rona hated. The vibrator she loved. Both sets of *Jerry's* BIG SAVINGS *Appliances* books. A plain paper bag that contained the jewelry he had removed from Rona's case and which was almost as valuable as he had told her they were when he gave them to her.

Then he looked around for a stuffed toy penguin with a yellow rubber beak that glowed in the dark and a foot that unscrewed and concealed a secret cavity where he kept a little something (supplied by Bobbi) that made him not care which way his head was screwed on.

The stuffed toy penguin was gone!

WHAT KIND OF FILTHY SNEAKING LOWLIFE SLIME WOULD KIDNAP A STUFFED TOY PENGUIN WITH A YELLOW RUBBER BEAK THAT GLOWS IN THE DARK?

So Jerry went into Rona's room (wincing as he heard her singing "The Girl from Ipanema" in the shower), saw the stuffed toy penguin with the yellow rubber beak that glowed in the dark lying beside her suitcase (the significance of the suitcase not registering on his kidnapped penguin-grieving plus scotch-steeped brain), nodded as he picked up her eyeglasses and dropped them out the window, cradled the stuffed penguin in his arms, and returned with dignity to his room, only falling down once. Then he had another scotch to celebrate the reunion of a man and his penguin. Tears welled.

*   *   *

Bobbi Whittier had had *enough!* No more *hinting!* No more *subtle! She was going in!* She hitched up her adorably sassy lemon-yellow tennis skirt. She tightened her cruel cruel Ninja-black halter. She clutched her tennis racket between her perfect white teeth as if it were a pirate's cutlass. She was going to bring back that Porsche dead or alive! Or at least no more than two years old and with less than twenty-five thousand miles on it.

She opened the Durants' sliding patio door (which Jerry had been too unscrewed to remember to lock) and stalked.

The hell with it!

Eddie Spang, city burglar moonlighting in the suburbs, had been assaulted by bushes, mosquitoes, crickets, moths, and various other Unidentified Flying and Non-Flying (goddamn crawling) Objects.

Now he had been slimed by a SLUG.

By God, he was going to rip off everything these barbarians had that was worth more than nine ninety-eight. People who keep slugs deserve everything they get.

Eddie patted his chrome-plated .25 (wimpy and gaudy but his mother had given it to him for his fourteenth birthday and it was the thought that counted) and went in through a first-floor side window that he found unlocked. (*Suburbanites!*)

Inside: TOTAL DARKNESS.

Do these suckers use *blackout curtains?*

Eddie flicked on his flashlight.

GERONIMO!

On the street Barry Frisbie parked his red Fiero and bounced up to the Durants' front door. He looked mostly great. His blond hair glowed in the dark *and* curled naturally in the dark. He also had a dazzlingly white-toothed smile and an I.Q. that Rona considered nearly as high as his dental count. And he had at *least* thirty-two teeth.

Tonight, however, he looked mostly great instead of absolutely great because he was frowning. Rona's phone call had thrown his forehead into unsightly wrinkling perturbation and had penetrated all the way into his brain. Those RABIES

SHOTS. Was Rona kidding? Or *not kidding?* That kind of thing wasn't anything to kid about. Rabies could ruin his tennis game. Maybe even his sex life.

Barry found the Durants' front door unlocked. He stepped inside the house, into a hall.

Dark. Very dark.

He took a right and a left.

Bobbi took a left and a right.

Eddie Spang took a Sony Compact Disk Player and a Panasonic Camcorder. And a cordless telephone and a five and a half inch color television plus radio.

He wasn't alone.

Barry Frisbie squinted into the darkness.

Someone. Someone not moving. Like him. But someone panting.

Sexy panting.

Rona?

Barry reached his hand out, tentatively, hopefully.

His hand encountered a pair of buttocks.

Well, great.

Sliding higher, his definitely hopeful hand stroked a pair of—

Great!

And, climbing higher, a tennis racket raised overhead in a smash position.

Gee. Neat form. Rona was really getting the hang of it.

Barry whispered: "Have you had your rabies shot?"

"What?" came a return whisper.

Barry said, "Woof, woof."

"You slimy barking cheapo creep!"

The tennis racket hit him on top of the head.

Barry hit the floor.

Bobbi said, "Don't think you can get out of a Porsche by lying there." She added, "And moaning." She continued, "Give me Porsche." She kicked him and amplified, "Jerry, I want a Porsche." She spelled it out, "P-O-R-S-C-H-E." She calmed down and started kicking him with the other foot, "Will *Jer-ree* give his sweetsie-sweetsie a Porschie-Worschie?" She growled and said, "Will the evil perverted whimpering slob give me a Porsche?" She said, enjoying herself now, *"Gimme Porsche."*

Rona Durant cocked her head alertly.

What's that noise?

There it was again.

BURGLAR!

Rona clenched her jaw, looked around—where the hell were her eyeglasses?—picked up an umbrella, and looked every inch Heidi the Hun.

A *squinting* Heidi the Hun. "I'll get the sneaking bastard."

She crept stealthily down the stairs. Feeling her way. She couldn't see a thing. Not in the dark and without her glasses.

But near the foot of the stairs she heard something. *A woman's voice.* A woman's voice talking to Rona's husband.

"Jerry, give me—"

And deep-throated animalistic male moaning.

RIGHT IN HER OWN HOUSE!

Rona changed direction and tiptoed for the living room. Burglars were one thing, husbands another. She wanted something heavier than an umbrella for husbands. She headed for the fireplace and the iron poker.

I'll kill the bastard!

In the dark Jerry Durant came down the stairs looking for a drink.

In the dark Eddie Spang came out of a looted room looking for another room to loot.

In the dark Rona Durant came looking for her husband.

"Gaaaaahhhhhh!" said Eddie Spang, bumping into someone in the dark and dropping his flashlight, which flicked off.

"Aaaaarrrrgggghhhh!" said Rona Durant, the bumpee. The attacking bumpee. Rona the Righteous Defender of Hearth and Home Against the Rotten Criminal Element. That is, her husband.

Wait till she got her hands on the thug!

Rona got her hands on the thug. Also her legs. It seemed to Eddie Spang like all four hands and certainly a good half dozen legs. He crashed to the floor with the flying octopus on top of him.

Fortunately for Eddie, Rona had dropped her fireplace poker in all the sudden athletic activity. Unfortunately for Eddie, she still had her shoes.

Sitting on top of Eddie in the almost total darkness, she proceeded to hammer the back of his head with the heel of one of her shoes—briskly, but without hurry, like a carpenter pounding tenpenny nails.

She said, "It's Slut Time, eh?" *Swat*. She said, "That Overdeveloped Omelet Brained Cokehead Next Door, eh?" *Whack*. She added, squinting, "How blind do you think I am, eh?" *Wham*. She continued, "Want to turn over and let me do the other side, eh?" *Rap*. "This one's getting a little soft." *Crash*.

Eddie Spang groaned.

"Darling, what are you trying to say?"

Boom.

Jerry Durant, decanter in hand, wobbled in what he vaguely believed was the general direction of the stairs, only falling down once.

Suddenly he paused.

He heard a man's groans. After several seconds he decided they weren't *his* groans.

And then he heard Rona's voice: "Darling, what are you trying to say?"

His wife and another man!

Well. Well. Well.

Unsteadily Jerry Durant fumble-felt his way along the hall to the stairs. Carefully he set the decanter on a step. He rolled his sleeves up. *Damn the Torpedoes. Don't Tread on Me.* THE BIGGER THEY ARE THE HARDER THEY FALL.

Jerry adopted a shaky wrestler's stance and began to advance crablike on where he judged his ruthless and cunning opponent to be in the darkness.

*   *   *

"This is no *fun* any more!" pouted Bobbi Whittier. Besides, both her feet were getting tired from kicking. So she stopped kicking the wretch lying at her feet in the darkness.

It showed what a party poop Jerry was these days. He just lay there and whimpered. Maybe he was some sickening weirdo masochist and enjoyed being hit by a tennis racket and kicked by expensive tennis shoes? Well, she'd punish the whimpering little sicko by *not* punishing him.

Bobbi said adultly, "We'll discuss this like two adults when you've stopped enjoying yourself in this disgusting way, Jerr. But let me say—you need *help*. And just let me add—I need a *Porsche*."

With a haughty toss of her hair, Bobbi headed for what she thought was the patio door.

But . . .

"Last of the Mohicans!"

With a belch of pure rage, Jerry Durant took a flying leap at the figure in the dark. Jerry Durant: HUSBAND FROM HELL!

Since the figure's back was to him, he couldn't see the perfect hair and perfect teeth that glowed in the dark and the perfect knockers that who gave a damn if they didn't glow in the dark.

"The Hell with the Alimony!"

Jerry threw at her everything in his old high school wrestler's repertoire. The *Hammerlock*. His ruthless and sneaky opponent said, "Wow." The good old *Grapevine*. She commented, "Kinky!" *The Bar Arm*. She chirped, "MORE!" The absolutely merciless and never-fail *Chicken Wing*. She hissed, "A little lower."

Jerry quickly ran out of steam. And he wasn't getting anywhere. She was enjoying this a lot more than he was. Killing Rona was just like having sex with her.

"Well, for Christ's sake," Jerry said, and lumbered to his feet. He needed a drink.

He stumbled away in the dark, only falling down once.

"YOU FILTHY BRUTAL TOTALLY DEPRAVED DIS-

GUSTING LOWLIFE DEGENERATE UNREAL ANI-
MAL!" Bobbi called after him.

When he didn't come back, she said, "Jerr?" She scrambled
to her feet. She called, "Wait for me!"

Bobbi lurched into the darkness, in pursuit of a sick mind
she could call her own.

She bumped into a door, fumbled it open, and lunged
through it.

Only it was the door to the basement stairs.

Bobbi said:

"WWWWWoooowww—!"

Falling.

Mrs. Edith Pyp, a next door neighbor of the Durants', telephoned the police. She wanted to report an excessively noisy
party.

A group of people were having a good time *and with all the
lights off!*

Landsakes!

Barry Frisbie was confused. He was conscious and he was
confused. Barely conscious. Deeply confused. Even for Barry,
who was certain about few things in life except his forehand
and his tan.

All he could remember was that he had been attacked by
Rona. His Rona baby. Attacked with a good graphite tennis
racket and a pair of sturdy-sole but chic tennis shoes. Also
aced by a really neat overhead smash.

Why? Why? Why?

It had something to do with rabies. That much he remembered.

Rabies.

Rona has *rabies*. Of course!

That explained it. The sudden mood swings, the irritability,
the restlessness. Probably water buildup, too.

He had heard of that. On Donahue. *The Pre-Rabies Syn-
drome.*

She had been too embarrassed to tell him. She had finally
just burst out like that. Just exploded.

Typical of rabies, of course. He nodded understandingly, Donahueishly.

Poor rabid honeybunch.

He would show her he wasn't just a stupid insensitive macho fabulously handsome jock with a great forehand and a really super tan. He'd show her he knew how to relate to a liberated, *today* woman.

Jesus Christ!

Jerry Durant nearly dropped the decanter.

In the darkness, something had grabbed his legs. Something had fallen on its knees and was pleading, its arms wrapped around Jerry's legs.

"Darling, it doesn't matter if you have rabies," the something whimpered.

At Jerry's feet sobbing noises were going on! Pressing-its-wet-nose-against-his-pants noises! *Kissing* noises!

Jerry froze. *Rona!* A dementedly lust-crazed Rona. An absolutely off her rocker Rona. My God, even her *voice* had changed!

"Bite me! Bite me! I don't care! I don't care!"

Good God! The BITCH!

Gaaaahhhh!

Jerry swung the decanter frantically in the darkness.

Rona Durant crept down the basement stairs in the dark, squinting. Something odd was going on in the house. A girl needed a baseball bat. Or a lead pipe. A shovel, at least.

Why am I in the dark in the *basement?* she suddenly asked herself.

Rona turned on the stairs light.

She quickly turned the light off.

There was a body lying at the bottom of the stairs.

She turned the light back on.

Bobbi Whittier.

Instantly Rona saw the headline: "WOMAN ARRESTED FOR BASHING HUBBIE'S TEEN TOOTSIE."

It would ruin her chances for alimony, her tennis game, her hair and nails for ten-to-fifteen years, even with a parole! The beauty salons alone in women's prisons must be sheer taste-less hells, judging from the way those women cons looked on *60 Minutes.*

Five minutes later Rona had dragged Bobbi into the garage, to Rona's Cadillac, heaved her onto the floor of the back seat, and thrown an old sheet over her.

Breathing heavily, Rona tiptoed back upstairs to get her car keys.

This place was a madhouse!

Eddie Spang felt his head—Holy Jesus: it was covered with *lumps!* It felt as if tenpenny nails had been hammered into his skull.

What the hell had happened?

He had broken into an insane asylum! It was the only logical explanation. A joint full of psycho wackos. Axe murderers. Norman Bates-types.

The thing that had jumped on him in the dark and called him a "slut" wasn't even *human.*

He had to get out of here. Fast. Before the THING came back.

Where was his loot? The *hell* with his loot! He'd take the first thing he could grab in the goddamn dark and beat it.

He didn't even notice that the thing he grabbed in the dark had a rubber beak.

A yellow rubber beak that glowed in the dark.

Jerry Durant discovered that smashing someone over the head with a decanter of whiskey was a sobering experience. Even if that someone was your sex-crazed Scandinavian bimbo wrestler lookalike wife.

God, he felt *terrible* about that whisky! He could hear it dripping in the dark.

He fumbled for the hall light switch. The lights came on.

He saw it wasn't only whisky that was dripping.

It also wasn't his sex-crazed Scandinavian bimbo wrestler lookalike wife.

He had seen the guy somewhere before. There was a tennis racket nearby. Also bits of racket stringing clung to his naturally curly hair and around his ears and shoulders. Tennis . . . *the assistant pro at the club!* Barry something. The one who worked on Rona's forehand. The one who . . .

Jerry suddenly saw it all: "MAN SMASHES WIFE'S SERVER." My God—ten to fifteen years in prison, even with a parole! He couldn't keep up his bookkeeping—*both* books. They had become a kind of hobby for Jerry. Almost an art form.

Five minutes later he finished lifting the sex-crazed non-Scandinavian tennis player into the trunk of Rona's Cadillac (Jerry's Mercedes was in the repair shop), tossed a blanket over him, and shut the trunk lid, only falling down once.

He then went out through the garage's side door and started shambling down the long driveway towards the road.

He needed some fresh air before he did anything more. He also needed a drink.

Rona Durant, having gone to her room and combed and lip-sticked, gotten her purse and car keys, and picked up her suit-case and a plain but stunning length of metal pipe she had found in the garage in case she saw her husband, tiptoed down the stairs to the first floor.

Where she saw her husband.

Or rather she saw a dark form skulking in a typically husbandly way while carrying a yellow beak that glowed in the dark.

"GIVE ME THAT PENGUIN!" she roared.

Another one! thought Eddie. He grabbed for his chromed .25.

"You filthy slimy inhuman rat-faced penguin-stealing *thief!*" bellowed Rona. She grabbed for her metal pipe.

Holy Jesus, thought Eddie, I recognize that voice! THE MAD HAMMERER! *I'll get a medal if I drop this wacko!* He whipped his gun out of his waistband and swiveled it (GOD-THIS-IS-GREAT!) Dirty Harry-ishly in the direction of the dark stairs and the hulking charging shape. And then Eddie shouted, "Eat lead, psycho!" and—*whoops*—flung the pistol at Rona's little toe.

There was a cry of pain in the darkness.

Then a roar: *"Wife-beater!"*
Something hit Eddie on the top of his head. Not for the first time in this house. But definitely for the last time.

Rona thought: Where the hell is Barry? He should've been here by now. Do I have to do everything by myself?

By herself Rona put what she thought was her filthy slimy inhuman rat-faced penguin-stealing husband's body in the Cadillac's back seat, on top of Bobbi Whittier.

After she shut the car door she remembered her spare eyeglasses in the Cadillac's glove compartment.

She opened the garage door, got in the driver's seat, put on the spare glasses (*Thank God*—she felt she had been stumbling around half blind all night) and drove down the highway.

Jerry had walked for MILES. Two blocks at *least*. Thirsty and dazed he lurched under a bright street light.
Screech!
A Cadillac slammed to a halt a few feet past him.
My God, that's lucky! He could use a lift.
Jerry opened the front passenger door and climbed in.
"YOU'RE NOT DEAD!"
Rona Durant stared horrified at Jerry Durant.
"YOU'VE GOT RABIES!"
Jerry Durant stared horrified at Rona Durant.
Jerry panicked and tried to open the passenger door. Rona panicked and hit the accelerator pedal.
The Cadillac weaved from side to side down the road, its two occupants trying to escape and punch each other's teeth out at the same time.

The police car—only thirty-five minutes after receiving the telephone call—was responding to Mrs. Pyp's report on loud behavior at the Durants' home.

The car and its two officers were two blocks from the Durants' neighborhood when they spotted loud behavior in an automobile. A careening, weaving Cadillac. A *riot* in an automobile.

Siren whining, they chased it down.

They were assisted in their lawful pursuit by a volunteer telephone pole which got in Rona's way.

The Cadillac stopped abruptly. The hood sprang open. The back doors flew wide. Also the trunk popped up.

When the police car screeched to a halt behind the Cadillac, a wild-eyed man reeking of alcohol also popped out of the Cadillac.

"She's trying to kill me again! First she tried to bite me, then she tried to hit me with a telephone pole!"

Jerry Durant staggered a few feet toward the policemen.

Something with a yellow rubber beak that glowed in the dark came *whooshing* out through the driver's window.

It hit Jerry in the back.

He dropped with a hoarse scream.

"*All right*," Jerry sobbed, face down in the road, his voice mingling rage, terror, and drunken dementia, "Bite me, bite me! I just don't care! I don't *care* if you've got rabies!"

One of the cops said: "Rabies?"

The other cop stared into the Cadillac's trunk and then into the back seat: "Jesus Christ!"

Jerry whispered: "Watch out for her teeth."

The first cop repeated: "RABIES?"

The penguin's yellow beak glowed . . .

"*Sunufabitch!*"

"Get her, get her, GET HER!" both cops yelled at the same time, grabbing for their guns.

BANG! BANG! BANG! BANG!

They riddled the stuffed toy penguin full of lead.

THE LOST DOG

ISAAC ASIMOV

The conversation had turned to pets, and both Jennings and Baranov were overflowing with wonder-tales of pets they had owned or had known.

I, as a non-pet person, was more than a little annoyed. Having no stories of my own to contribute, I occupied myself in pooh-poohing theirs. I denied that dogs had human intelligence, that horses were gifted with telepathy, and that cats had a sly wisdom that routed their owners every time.

I was sneered at, of course, and finally out of sheer desperation I called on Griswold for help. He, to all appearances, had been sleeping soundly throughout the sometimes heated discussion, but I never doubted his capacity to know what was going on despite any state of unconsciousness he might appear to be immersed in.

"Griswold," I said, "did you ever encounter any superhuman animals?"

Griswold's ice-blue eyes opened and one of his formidable eyebrows lifted sardonically. He sipped at the Scotch-and-soda he had been holding firmly in his hand and said, "I found a dog once."

"A wonder-dog?" I asked suspiciously.

"No," he said, "just an ordinary, nondescript mutt."

"If he's not a wonder-dog," I said, "then the argument is settled. If, with your imagination, you can't claim you were involved with a wonder-dog, then I maintain there aren't any."

"This dog—" said Griswold.

"That's all right," I said, waving my hand at him negligently. "We don't need the story."

This dog [said Griswold] was brought to my attention by Katherine Adelman, a nurse with whom I had been rather friendly in times past. What's more, I still had some youthful fire in me—this was several decades ago—and I was sentimental enough to be willing to listen to her, even though at that time, as I recall, I had much of greater moment to occupy my mind.

She told me there was a man dying in one of her wards and she was very upset over it.

"I'm sorry," I said mechanically, though I knew she must encounter death every day, it could be no stranger to her.

"He's a derelict," she said. "He was picked up on the street and brought in. We know practically nothing about him, except part of his name. When we asked him his name, he managed a strangled 'Jeff.' That was all he ever said. After that he just lay there, barely conscious, and then he slipped off into a kind of semi-coma."

"Is he being well treated?" I asked—a bit sardonically. The hospital, after all, however high-minded its ideals might be, subsisted on money, and coddling a dying derelict must go against the grain.

"Of course," she said, with a touch of reproach. And then, showing that she quite understood the point I was making, she added, "He won't be much of an expense. He'll be dead in a day or two."

You must understand that in those days the medical profession was not quite as well equipped with devices to keep the soul within the body against the body's will. People died more speedily and easily, and with greater dignity.

I said, "Why are you concerned, Kate, aside from your general disapproval of death?"

"It's a little thing. As I told you, he was found on the street, and I'm sure he'd gone out, sick as he was, squandering his last strength in the cold and the wet in order to try to find his dog." There were tears in her eyes, and I grew uneasy. She was an ardent dog-lover—that had been an important factor in spoiling our pleasant relationship—and I knew that the matter of the dog would weigh far more heavily with her than anything else would. She was going to ask me to do something, and I might not be able to refuse.

I said, "Did he tell you so?"

"No. He was past talking, as I said, but he managed to scrawl a note on a piece of paper I brought him for the purpose."

"I presume you also brought him a pen."

"Yes, and a board to write on."

"How did you know he wanted all that?"

"He was trying to talk and failing. He could only wheeze and cough in a most pathetic way, and when he made weak but desperate writing gestures it was obvious what he wanted. I've dealt with so many dying people, Griswold, I can almost read their minds."

I nodded. "I'm guessing you have the note with you and that you want me to look at it."

"Yes, I do," she said, and showed me a scrap of paper. "He went into the semi-coma while he was writing it."

I don't have that piece of paper to show to you, and I rather despair of reproducing the exact wording, orthography, and handwriting, but I shall use the amenities of the Union Club library to produce something that will be close enough for the purpose.

PLEEZ MY DORG WAZ
TAKEN TO THE POND GET
IT FOR ME PLEEZ I CANT
DAY WITHOUT I SAY GOODBY
IT ANSERS TO ITS NAME
WHICH IS

Kate was weeping by now. She said, "He must have been too sick to prevent his dog—unlicensed, I'm sure—from being taken away. I suppose he gathered his last strength to go to the pound to retrieve his dog and then collapsed en route."

I said, "And you haven't been able to find out anything about him? Has he any friends?"

She shook her head. "He's just a derelict. He doesn't live in this area. Neither the police nor the people at the local soup-kitchen recognize him. He may be utterly homeless, living out of garbage cans, with nothing but his dog for company. His clothes were rags and he had no effects—certainly no money. I suppose if we ran a full investigation we might find out something, but that's not important. What I need to do is get his dog."

"What good would that do?" I asked gloomily.

"He killed himself trying to get that dog, Griswold, and now he's going to die utterly alone. No one should die alone."

"Many people have to," I said, trying to console her and feeling that I was only sounding heartless. "Can you get the dog?"

"I went to the pound this morning," she said. "I didn't know exactly when they'd picked up the dog and they couldn't iden-tify any as belonging to a particular dying derelict. They knew nothing about it. They just picked up unlicensed dogs and they had over a dozen—it seemed like a hundred to me. I wanted to take them all and bring them to the poor man. If he woke up, he'd know if one were his. But of course I could never bring that horde of dogs to his room. I'd be lucky to smuggle in *one*."

"You'd be risking your job."

"I know. But which one would it be? All I knew was that it would answer to its name. But he never managed to finish the note and write its name. —Did you ever read *Rumpelstiltskin*, Griswold?"

"Of course," I said. "When I was a child."

"I felt like the princess who was going to lose her baby to the evil little dwarf unless she could guess his name. Except that she had a year to do the guessing and I had only an hour or so. I just kept calling out, 'Rex,' 'Fido,' 'Spot'—every doggy name I could think of—and got nowhere. Some dogs barked and yelped and ran about, but they weren't responding to some particular name."

"You don't even know if the dog is male or female, do you?"

"No. But after I called Rex I tried Regina, and after I called Prince I tried Princess. I tried ordinary names—Bill and Jane, for instance. I tried Curly and Genevieve." She looked at me and tried to smile. "I even tried Rumpelstiltskin."

I said, "I take it that didn't work."

"No. Nothing worked. I finally had to give up."

I said, "You know, Kate, the dog may have been put down."

"Oh, *no,*" she said, in obvious pain, "they keep it for several days in case the owner shows up, or someone wants it." Then she said, "I suppose that no one *would* want it, though. I keep thinking that that penniless old man must have had a penniless old dog, if you know what I mean. Their love for each other was the only possession in all the world that either of them had. —And I must do something about it."

I nodded. She was a soft-hearted girl. It wasn't her fault that the world had failed to turn her cynical.

She said, "So I came to you."

"What can I do?"

"Won't you come to the pound with me now? I still have a couple of hours before my work-shift begins."

"I can do that if I have to, but what else can I do?"

"You may be able to think of a name I couldn't think of. Or you may be able to tell which dog is the derelict's just by looking at it. You know how clever you are."

I said, "I'm not clever enough to pluck a name out of thin air, Kate. Even the princess only got the dwarf's name because she overheard him announce it."

But the tears were rolling quietly down her cheeks—and she *was* pretty, and I was quite young, and the memories I had did their mischief. I said, "Well, let me think."

She waited for me, watching with her big, trusting eyes, and that gave me no choice. I said, "Very well, let's go to the pound."

We went there and were taken to the department of recent acquisitions, if I might call it that. It smelled and it was noisy and I didn't like it. It was the first time I'd ever visited a pound, as it happened.

I slapped my knees and called out a name—and one of the dogs went wild. He yelped happily and threw himself at the mesh barrier trying to get at me, with his tail wagging into a blur.

I said to the attendant in charge, "I want that dog. I belongs to a friend of mine. I'll pay for the license and any other fee required, but I must have it now. My friend is dying."

Kate was wearing her nurse's uniform. She presented her hospital badge with her photograph and confirmed that it was life and death, and we got the dog.

We raced to the hospital and, with a sympathetic doctor, and quite against the hospital rules, we smuggled the dog into the room in which its master lay dying.

The dog emitted a muffled whine and nuzzled the derelict's hand. The dying man's eyes opened at the touch, and his head turned slightly. He could do no more than smile faintly and his hand trembled as he reached out to pat the dog's head just once. He died, then, with his only friend licking his hand.

Afterward, Kate took the dog away, much against its will. She left it in my charge, but at the end of her shift she took it over and adopted it.

The dog died a year afterward and, eventually, so did Kate. It was I who sat at her bedside and made certain that she didn't die alone, either.

Griswold's eyes were blinking as he finished his drink, and he rubbed his nose rather violently.

We did not speak for a while but then Jennings said softly, "But how did you come to know the dog's name?"

Griswold said, "It was just a guess. The only thing we knew about the man was that his name was Jeff. I had to ask myself what someone named Jeff would call his dog if the dog was a shaggy, nondescript, unkempt mongrel. Well, there was once a comic strip that maintained its popularity over half a century or more called *Mutt and Jeff*. Augustus Mutt was a human character in the strip, but might it not occur to someone named Jeff who owned a mutt to call him Mutt in honor of the strip?

It was a long chance, but with Kate looking at me I had to try."

I said sardonically, "A long chance indeed."

"Not for you three," growled Griswold. "As soon as I mentioned the dog, I described him as an ordinary, nondescript mutt, remember? How much more of a hint did you want?"

THE MYSTERY OF
THE MISSING MARSUPIAL

ROBERT HALSTED

"Maybe we could have an *après*-hurricane party?" Millie suggested.

I thought for a moment. "Great idea, but we might get more return invitations than we could handle."

"You mean other people are digging out of the ruins, too?"

"That's the local custom."

Nadya had been rough on us, though we had it relatively easy considering the people who didn't have homes to come back to or, worse, vice versa. The cottage was still standing, and there was very little—a couple of cheap pieces of furniture and some odds and ends—that was so far gone we had to throw it out. We'd still be discovering mummified marine specimens under things for a while, but we had basic cleanup fairly well done.

"But some kind of recreational break is indicated," I continued the thought. "How about lunch at the Burger Palace, or a *brief,* my feet are already killing me, shopping tour?"

"Great! As soon as I finish laundering our drug money."

We'd actually, if you can imagine it, forgotten the several thousand dollars we'd rescued from a watery grave in the Gulf of Mexico until we started cleaning up. We tried to see it less as a windfall than as a backup system. If we spent much at a time there'd be a lot of bureaucrats asking questions and grabbing percentages we didn't really think belonged to them—

Millie and I both have a healthy anarchist streak—so we put it in a hidey-hole for gradual and/or emergency use.

After Nadya, we noticed the beginnings of deterioration, so we decided on a mild bleach to kill the mildew, followed by a clearwater rinse and sun drying. Millie, who was just learning domesticity—she'd never even made her own bed till she went to college—even ironed a few bills, but it made them look too good. Slightly shabby is more anonymous.

So I pitched in, and soon we had them neatly bundled. This time we stowed them upstairs, in the back of my studio filing cabinet. Since the bundles didn't come out even, we impulsively held back a few bills for a spending spree.

We ate a couple of notches better than the Burger Palace, at a little mom-and-pop place I'd recently discovered in Palm City called the Metropole. Their daily special might vary from Tex-Mex to Dixie grease-grits-and-gravy to something approaching Continental *haute cuisine*. Today it was a Creole concoction on rice, and quite decent.

"Someday I'll be a culinary genius and you'll be proud of me," Millie volunteered over butterscotch pudding.

"I'm already proud of you, darling," I responded. Not out of any gallantry but because I was proud of her. I feel ennobled and ornamented by her presence. If not by her cooking, so far and mostly.

Resurfacing after following her own underground train of thought, she said, "I think the vegetable garden is most urgent."

We'd lost nearly all our young winter veggies in the storm, and this had been a crushing blow for her. I think Millie's tear ducts are hooked up wrong. She takes major disasters with a smile and weeps copiously at small, easily corrected things like having to replant. Which Florida farmers have to do two winters out of three in the normal course of events. I think she may have had a personal relationship with each plant.

"But you have to give me moral support. I'm afraid of Stetson."

"?"

"I was a morbid child. I read Eliot in college. On purpose."

"Ugh. You mean 'The corpse you planted in your garden'?

But I think we got them all. There was only ol' Bill, that we knew of, and we located him. Anybody else would be just nice neat bones by now, what with all the crabs and buzzards and things."

"Nonetheless, your moral support is required. And your strong back."

So instead of finery and baubles, we shopped for vegetable plants. We weren't the first ones to think of replanting, and it was a seller's market. The fashion and glamor stuff would have been cheaper. After tracking all over Palm City and suburbs, we found most of what we wanted in pots or six-packs for quick results, and the rest in packets to grow the slow, natural way. We got some extra to pot for replacements as needed.

My kitchen garden, though it has yet to reach the full flower of its gardenhood, so to speak, is highly superior by coastal Florida standards. On the site of the original kitchen garden for the Big House, it has been enriched over the decades with leaf rakings and grass clippings. I've put my kitchen compost there and kept the humus from leaching out by always having it planted or mulched. The storm had done it no good, but it was still fair soil, and the rain had leached out the salt from high-tide flooding. Even the dry season was no problem, with a pump and sprinklers hooked up to a salt-free flowing well.

Thus it was with a right good will and cheerful optimism that we set about replanting. Within a couple of days we had a handsome, sizable, and recognizable veggie patch. What Millie lacked in horticultural experience she made up in enthusiasm, neatness, and a sense of procedural thoroughness. We were both proud of it.

Millie, of course, had to check every day. I half expected to catch her measuring the tomato plants or ever so carefully digging up radish seeds to see if they'd sprouted. I checked less often, having learned by experience that plant growth is more impressive seen once or twice a week instead of every morning and evening.

*   *   *

Before too long, our surviving peppers and tomatoes had young fruits on them, and all our seedlings were growing nicely.

Then one Tuesday morning, Millie came in fit to be tied. Just about literally. Her tears of pain approached despair, her tears of anger verged upon rage.

It would be unwise to attempt a summary, or perhaps more fairly a translation, of what she said. I believe she would have clawed the eyes out of a culprit or even a half-decent suspect. When she simmered down to near coherence, I was able to extract the information that our new-made garden had been savaged. By then it had been looking like a real, if not quite harvestable, garden, and I too was upset. Though not to the same degree.

She took me by the hand and led me out for an eyewitness view. It really did look a mess, though my skilled gardener's eye told me that the actual loss was not as serious as it had seemed at first sight. The tomatoes and peppers were mostly flattened but basically intact, and could be restaked. Some of the Bibb lettuce and wong bok were totally missing, and others sort of two-dimensional.

Urging her to a more rational view, I quoted, "Come, let us reason together."

"Don't say 'lettuce,' it breaks my heart."

I didn't expect to find any evidence to identify the vandal or vandals. No comprehensible motive, of course, is required for vandalism, so any clues would pretty well have to be physical, and I thought I wouldn't find any.

Well, I was right and I was wrong. There was evidence all over, but we couldn't make head nor tail of it. Literally, as it turned out.

Some of the plants were untouched, some were mashed flat, some were pulled up by the roots, others looked as if they'd been chopped or shredded. The mulch was disturbed, but not in any recognizable pattern—in places it was pushed aside in windrows, elsewhere it looked as if a great chicken had scratched it, and here and there were deep depressions that looked as if somebody had dropped a sandbag or a drunk had passed out and fallen headlong.

"Applying my deductive facilities, Whatsit—" I began.

"You mean 'faculties,' Mr. Bones."

"Whatever. If you're gonna murder the culprit, you may need to apply for an EPA permit."

"You mean . . ."

"I fear, Whatsit, that no human agency has done this deed."

"Well, if it's an animal, I'm not quite as mad as I was, but I'm still mad. What kind?"

"Well, I'm not really sure. Maybe something out of medieval bestiary. Sometimes it ploughs, and sometimes it chops." I showed her the various kinds of damage, and we tried to design a creature to do the job. It looked something like an elephant on swamp-buggy wheels, with sharp fangs.

She examined one of the depressions in the soft sand. "I say, Bones, is this a pugmark I see?"

"Pugmark?"

"You read about them in lion and tiger books. Maybe only big cats have pugs."

I looked at the spot. There did seem to be toe-shaped marks at the forward end of the sunken area. "Think a panther did it?"

"Why not?"

I measured the putative pugmark with my eye.

"One reason why not, Whatchername—"

"Whatsit."

"One reason why not, Whatsit, is that such a panther would have to be, at my estimate, some seven feet, or twenty-one hands, high at the shoulder. Say a little under ten meters, tip to tip, or about thirty feet. And would weigh a good eighty stone."

"How much is a stone?"

"Twelve pounds, or maybe fourteen. I forget."

"Maybe a really big Bengal tiger?"

"I sincerely hope not. Besides, I'm sure it ate some cabbage."

"And Bengal tigers eat Hindu peasants."

"Sometimes a Paki or two."

"H'm."

"Yeah."

We spent a while lining up jobs for the replanting project, but we wanted Jim Pierson to be our consulting detective on this one before we mucked up the evidence, so we didn't start yet. The *Mary Jo* was ringing, so we knew he wasn't out to sea, but we couldn't raise any hands aboard.

I had a job to get out, so I deserted Millie, who had other chores to do anyhow. We never did get hold of Jim. After supper we were both pretty tired, so we went to bed early, still intrigued and puzzled. Millie talked in her sleep, but I couldn't make any sense of it.

Next morning she was still zonked out when I woke, so I built a pot of coffee but held off breakfast.

"I had an awful nightmare," she said when she finally drifted in. "I was in Australia. I was coming back from the grocery store and this huge terrible beast was trying to catch me and steal my groceries—"

We looked at each other. It took us three or four seconds each before our cerebral computers shuffled through their card files.

"What do kang—" I began.

"Kangaroo!" she said simultaneously.

Clad in our kimonos or less, we dashed out into the chilly-enough subtropical morn barefoot. In the slanting morning light all the tracks made sense: here was where the brute had leapt from point A to point B, that furrow was where he'd dragged his tail while munching on our greens. When we checked closely, all the stuff that was actually missing, not merely trampled, was edible foliage.

"Let's check the outback," Millie suggested.

We went round to the far edge where a low sand embankment shelters the garden from encroaching scrub and winter winds. Sure enough, there in a sandy spot was a clear-enough-to-read print of a foot nearly as long as my leg, well defined toes and all. I was glad it *wasn't* a tiger.

"Kangaroos sure do have big pugs," commented Millie.

"Gives 'em good understanding," I replied. She aimed a token kick at me with her bare, sandy foot.

Sam had been following us around, half spooked. When he sniffed the big print, he fuzzed up a bit and muttered a growl under his breath, then went back home as directly as he could without crossing kangaroo tracks.

After standing around in awe and wonder for a while, we migrated back to the cottage and started breakfast cooking. By the time we finished the last of the toast, we figured it was time to call in our consultant, so Millie rang the *Mary Jo*. The cap'n wasn't in, but Millie told Janie we needed help tracking down a kangaroo, figuring that would bring a quick return call from Jim.

Sure enough, in half an hour or less the phone rang, and it was Jim.

"Got a message from you, but my mate musta forgot to unscramble it," he announced without ceremony.

"Nope," I answered. "What you heard is what we said."

"Boy, if you'd drink normal beer like the rest of us instead of that fancy imported stuff, maybe your brain wouldn't burn out so quick."

"Cold sober, Y'r Honor," I answered. "I got a witness, and you can see the evidence for yourself."

"I will." He rang off, abruptly as usual. I've never known the man to say goodbye.

Millie and I went to dress, knowing he'd be so driven by curiosity we'd see him in fifteen minutes or less. It was just over twelve.

We took him on a royal tour of the mysterious spoor, pointing out the evidence as we went along and saving the clear track on the far side for a final exhibit. He maintained his poker face and usual stolid silence throughout. Finally, he said, "Damned if it don't look like a kangaroo."

After a major concession like that, he needed coffee, so we made another pot and sat around conferring.

"Offhand," he said at last, "I don't have a ready answer. Nothin' to do but start bird-doggin' around. Mind if I run up a phone bill?"

"Suit yourself. We'll take it out of the kangaroo reward money."

We stood around while he called, first, the local law authorities (without giving his name), then some wildlife exhibits in the area. Africa World hadn't lost a kangaroo. Nor had Tropical Park, nor Gulf Gardens. He even called a couple of circus headquarters up in Sarasota and got the same negative answer.

"There's something in the back of my mind," said Millie.

"At least we're sure it ain't in the front," retorted Jim. I no longer rose to her defense on these occasions, knowing she'd eventually make Jim pay double for any insults. For now, she just stuck out her tongue and continued.

"Something unofficial, that isn't supposed to be there. It has a funny name. Kind of like a church or a fraternity."

A nebulous recognition stirred in the back of my own mind. Somewhere in my mental attic, as in hers, the information existed, but rather than wait another overnight for elucidation I decided to call Bill Zeeman at the *Herald-Times*. I'd got to know him when I was doing some in-house freelancing for the paper, and we would help each other out from time to time. After a couple of attempts and some waiting, I got him on the line.

"Bill, ol' buddy, I got a question. Can you tell me the name of a guy who runs a sort of illegal wild animal farm?"

"Omega. The guy's name is . . . Seeger, Ed Seeger. That help?"

"Omega! Okay, that figures. I think it does help. How can I get hold of him?"

"He's way out in the toolies, off Indian Store Road. No phone. I can give you some rough directions." Which he did.

With very little preamble we piled into Jim's car and headed onto the mainland and northward up Indian Store Road. The directions Bill had given me weren't quite complete, but after a couple of wrong turns and asking directions we saw an odd-looking set of structures up ahead and smelt an elephanty sort of smell. I was hoping Millie wouldn't think of asking for some elephant manure to put on the garden.

We pulled up at the gate and piled out of the car. A sun-wrinkled guy with a Spanish-moss beard, somewhere between thirty-five and seventy, detached himself from a group of workers and came toward us.

"Sorry, folks, this is a workday. We'd like to be open full time, but right now we only have visitors on Sundays." He addressed himself to me, which is usual, since I was the tallest of our brigade.

"We're not exactly visitors. If you're Ed Seeger, we've come to talk with you about a problem with your animals."

Ed glanced over at Jim. Jim hasn't been a cop for twenty or thirty years, but he might as well wear a badge and uniform.

"Look, goddammit, I'm *trying* to conform. The last state guy out here, he gave me sixty days to get the pens up to code. The county man said I can do this on agricultural zoning, which is what I'm zoned. Right now I'm busting my butt just trying to keep these animals *alive*."

"But—" I began.

"And I'm trying to do it on no money at all. My savings are gone, and I'm working on volunteer contributions. If you government people want to get involved, you might get me a grant instead of sticking sticks in the spokes."

"But—"

"Every one of these animals would be dead if it weren't for me. See that pony over there? He was starving to death when I got him. That leopard has no claws and no fangs, and he was bleeding from whip lashes. Every one of 'em has been starved and abused and abandoned—"

Millie—whose eyes, as I knew they would be, were getting shiny with unshed tears, and her tenderheartedness is one of the reasons I adore and admire her—stepped forward and said in the middle of his tirade, "Are you missing a kangaroo?"

"Yes," he answered simply. "Have you seen it?"

"He's been in our garden, I think."

"She. Where's your garden?"

"Live Oak Key."

He frowned. "I don't think that's possible."

Jim stepped in. "You wanna see the tracks?"

Ed debated with himself for a moment. "Reckon I'd better." He called out to one of the laborers and turned to go with us.

Millie was petting a scared grey burro who'd come up to us. "Her name's Betty Boop," Ed told her. "Bring her a carrot next time, and you've got a friend for life."

Getting back to the cottage was quicker and easier than the trip out. We took Ed over to the garden and showed him the tracks. He looked, and nodded, and said mostly to himself, "Gotta be her. And she loves Chinese cabbage. Night before last, you say?"

We were nearly out of coffee grounds, so I was glad when he wanted to start tracking immediately instead of having a conference first. We showed him the lay of the land—the bay to the west and south; mostly scrub, a little farming, groves and houses to the north; so we decided to look eastward.

Live Oak Key is shaped sort of like Italy, or maybe the letter L. We're at the southwestern point, the tip of the heel. The inhabited part of the island is the upright, and toward the toe is basically wilderness, part state-owned wetlands and part development-prohibited private lands with no more than a few fishing camps on it. From our side there's a rough but usable-if-you-can-find-it land bridge among the mangroves. Nestled in the center of this area is a couple of hundred acres of surprising high and dry land, substantially unspoiled.

We figured that the animal would have been noticed if it had headed up-land and would have finished off our cabbage if it had stayed around the point. Assuming it didn't swim— and Ed was pretty sure it couldn't—it either was carried away, and no big vehicles had been by, or else it had to have headed east into the bush.

Millie did a quick change into long pants and sleeves and I put on a pair of socks, then we headed for the land bridge. When we got to a bare, sandy spot, Ed went ahead and looked close. Then he knelt down and beckoned us over. There in the sand was the same track Millie and I had seen in the garden, but clearer. It was headed eastward. "That's Susie," he said. "See that scar on the third toe?" We saw it.

I don't know whether Ed was an old bushtracker or was putting on an act for us, but he'd move on a couple of dozen paces, look around, sniff and listen, then change directions. Once he saw a dropping on the edge of the trail and said, "There's bear here," which surprised me. Another time I heard a gator gronking through a stand of cypress, and was as-

tounded at the amount of fresh-water habitat on our little bay
island. We'd have to come here with a camera some day.

All this time we'd been going through pine, cabbage palms,
cypress, and a little oak, with only the occasional white man-
grove. Then we felt the woods thinning out and saw a parklike
glade of savanna ahead. Ed motioned us to caution and silence, and strode ahead as we crept cautiously behind. He
stopped us at the edge of the glade, then slow-motioned us forward.

We looked over and around him, and there was probably the
first live kangaroo I'd ever seen (it's hard to separate child-
hood memories from Disney films). I was pretty impressed—
the brute was nearly as tall as Millie, and far heavier in the
hips. I'd say three or four hundred pounds of 'roo, as we old
outbackers call them in Stryne, our native tongue.

"Well?" asked Jim in a stage whisper.

"Wrong kangaroo," said Ed.

Our jaws dropped, and we stood there, speechless.

"Just jokin', folks. It's Susie. Y'all stay back here." He
went, one step at a time, out into the glade and began crooning
her name like a mother trying to lure a toddler back from the
edge of a high roof.

She caught sight of him, started, turned her head back toward him, and wiggled her ears comically. He took another
step or two forward, held out his hand, and continued talking.
Then she took a hop or two toward him, and finally they were
hugging in the middle of the clearing. He whispered confiden-
tial stuff in her ear, gave her a pat on the shoulder, and came
back toward us. She loped behind him for a couple of hops,
then saw us and stood stock-still.

"Not gonna be easy," he said when he got to us. "I'll get me
a crew together, and maybe we can lead her out with ropes.
I'll be back later today."

Jim had business to do, so Millie and I drove Ed back out to
Omega, where we got a brief tour and Millie realized the
dream of a lifetime by petting—cautiously—an old friendly
pussycat of a tiger. We learned that he called the place Omega
because it was the end of the line for its residents, a zoo of last

resort. It had started with a few exotic pets people had dumped on him, and grew from there.

While we would have enjoyed watching Susie brought home, there was a consensus that the fewer strangers the better, so Millie and I set to work in the garden, which didn't seem nearly so bad now. After lunch Ed and his crew came out with a homemade rig, a sort of mesh cage on a four-wheel trailer, and backed it as far into the woods east of the shell road as it would go. Then they set off down the trail.

No more than an hour later a four-wheel-drive pickup with state decals on the door pulled up and a big beefy guy with a real mother-banger of a rifle climbed out.

"Where's the kangaroo?" he demanded, looking through the woods at Ed's truck and trailer. I didn't get good vibes from him.

"Kangaroo?" I stalled. He just didn't feel like he was on our side, and I wanted him to go back where he came from.

"We got a report there was a dangerous kangaroo escaped down here destroying property and endangering life."

"I have no idea where any kangaroo is. We're having enough trouble with the goats," I lied.

"Goats?"

"Some idiot dumped a load of goats in our mangroves and the rancher's trying to round 'em up now." I wasn't sure whether I had him going or not.

"I'll just go check on it," the state man said, and headed toward the woods.

Millie had crept up on our blind side during this exchange. She stopped the guy in mid-stride by saying, "If you came to check on the bear, they've already taken it away."

"Bear?"

"The one they were using the goats as bait for. It was in the back of a station wagon. I don't know whether they shot it or just tranquilized it." I believe everything Millie tells me, but not some of the things she tells other people. Compulsively truthful people make fabulous liars when adequately motivated. They're used to being credible.

"When did they take it?"

"Just a little while ago. Maybe fifteen minutes."

"Did you say a station wagon?"

"Yes, a big blue one. A Ford or a Dodge, I think—a big American one. I meant to write down the license number, but I got distracted. It was four-WD-seven-something." She was looking at the chrome lettering on his fender when she said that.

He dug up our shell road turning around and zooming back north. As soon as he was out of sight, Millie and I raced into the woods to warn Ed, but they were already coming up the trail with Susie, leashed and compliant. We gave him a quick rundown, and he decided to get off the island as quickly as he could, before the wildlife ranger or whatever he was dropped the red herring and came back for the big fish. As it happened, we haven't seen the guy to this day—I hope he's still looking for the bear poachers and leaving other people's kangaroos alone.

The next day we drove out to Omega with Jim to see if Ed had got Susie home okay. When he saw us pull up, he came to the gate with a big smile on his face and led us back to the mesh-roofed pen that was Susie's domain.

We talked to the kangaroo and then drifted around visiting the other animals while Jim conferred with Ed. Eventually Jim ran out of questions, or maybe Ed ran out of time and patience, and we headed back home.

"Drop me off at the boat," Jim said. "I got some answers to track down."

Now, I'm curious—say, intellectually curious or idly curious—but Jim is compulsively curious.

He cannot share the world with an unsolved puzzle, an unanswered question, at least where anything like a crime is concerned. So far as I cared, Susie was back home and that was our purpose. I would always wonder how she got out of Omega, and more so how she got onto the island, but I wasn't going to let it interfere with the rest of my life.

After lunch, Millie and I got to discussing our back yard forest preserve and decided to use up some film. I loaded up with some Fujichrome 200, the fastest I care to shoot with out-

doors, and took along a longish lens in case we saw a panther
or something in the distance. I was sure there were none on the
island, but then I would have told you there were no bears or
kangaroos either.

I did mostly scenics—sweeps of beautiful Florida sky with
fantasy clouds over the treetops, a closeup of an air plant
blooming on a bald cypress, a strange ground-orchid, one twig
of autumn-colored oak that must've strayed down from up
North. I thought I saw a possum or coon up a tree, but it was
gone by the time I got rigged up. I decided after that to leave
the camera set for quick animal shots and readjust for things
that would stand fairly still, like trees and skies.

We were creeping up on the eye of the cypress head (that's
the pond in the middle), Millie leading the way since she's
much lighter on her feet than I am, when she gave an urgent
hand signal. I tiptoed up even with her and she whispered in
my ear, "It's not a gator, I don't know what it is."

I crept past her and got a glimpse of what seemed to be an
otter, unless it was a beaver, which I think we don't have
down here. I got two or three shots, including one in a reveal-
ing belly-up maneuver, before it submerged. After it failed to
reappear for several minutes, I did some sky-and-water studies
and we went on.

We were circling toward home when we came upon a de-
lightful glade nestled in amongst heavy woods. I was studying
angles to shoot it from when I saw a jarring note—something
didn't belong.

I swept my eyes slowly back over the scene, and there were
some wrong trees there. They were all about the same twelve
feet tall, the leaves were wrong, and the spacing was wrong—
they stood at almost regular intervals in a curving line at the
edge of the glade. The bark was peeling off in flakes, but they
weren't gumbo-limbo and it was the wrong time of year for
gumbo-limbo to peel. I walked up to one, broke off a leaf, and
tasted it.

"Ugh. Eucalyptus," I said spitting out the cough medicine-
tasting leaf. Eucalyptus grow here, but I've never seen them
naturalize like some of our other imports—the notorious pep-
pertree and the abominable cajeput. And I've never seen *any*

tree naturalize in an evenly spaced curving line that didn't fol
low a watercourse.

I dug with my fingers around the base of the tree, then
moved to a couple of the others and did the same thing.

"Behold, Whatsit," I cried to my puzzled comrade. "Perlite
vermiculite, and coarse northern peat, languishing here in the
Florida sand. Unless my eyes deceive me, someone has
planted exotic trees in this otherwise natural wilderness." I
went on to explain the clues that had led me to this conclusion

"Good show, Mr. Bones. Did you say eucalyptus? You
were sort of expectorating as you spoke."

"Eucalyptus indeed. And why here?"

"You mean why here instead of Borneo or California or
botanical gardens or wherever they're native to?"

"Aw—" I stopped myself. I'm sure my mouth hung open
and my eyes widened.

" 'Aw, shucks'?"

"No, I don't want to say it."

She got the same look of shocked insight on her face I must
have had on mine. "Can't be. Must be a coincidence. But
watch out for wild Abos on the warpath anyhow."

"I'd rather not talk about it." And actually we didn't, since
we were both processing the data and didn't have any results
to show yet. Millie did once in a while mumble through stiff
lips something like "Fair dinkum, Cobber," and once I found
myself whistling "Toy Me Kangaroo Down, Boys," but we re
frained from any direct reference while we finished our tour
and afterwards.

Next day I took the film to Russ at the One Hour Color Lab
in North Palm City, and the subject sort of faded into the background as Millie and I caught up on other jobs. I had a personally referred book illustration job I was doing for a friend of a
friend up North and I wanted to turn out an excellentissimo
job, so I was close-reading the copy chapter by chapter as she
sent it to me. For time spent, I was getting almost minimum
wage, but I figured it was a good investment in more ways
than one, and I was tied into royalties if it went over more than
medium-small.

When I went to mail the illustrations a day or two later, I stopped back by Russ's to pick up my slides and prints. I always shoot with a positive film and pay extra for negatives and prints, then carefully catalogue everything. Not because I'm an orderly person, but because I'm not.

"Where the hell have you *been?*" demanded Russ when I stepped into the shop.

"Oh, I've been tied up a couple of days on a job. I'm sorry if I held you up—I didn't know the processor was ever in a hurry."

"No, no—where were you shooting those rolls?"

"Far corner of Live Oak Key, sort of across the road from my house. Why do you ask?"

"You're lying, you crafty rascal. What d'you say about *this?*" He slapped an eight by ten print down on the counter. "I blew it up because I didn't believe it."

The enlarged detail was a little grainy and fuzzy, but you could see the otter clearly, except it did turn out to be a beaver. Except . . . when you looked closely at it it wasn't. The face was far too much like a duck's.

I've never passed out—that is, fainted—in my life, but I had a dizzy spell and actually blanked out for a moment. My computer tripped a breaker somewhere.

"Gee, Russ, what can I say? It must be that outdated film you sold me."

"That stuff was so fresh I wasn't supposed to sell it till two months after you bought it. Come on, I won't tell anybody."

"Russ, I promise you'll be among the first to know. Even if I have to call you at three o'clock in the morning. But first I have to find out myself. Meanwhile, could you keep mum?"

I usually jaw a while, but this time I paid up and walked out with Russ still throwing questions at me. It was all I could do to keep myself from stopping at *Mary Jo* as I passed by Shrimptown, but when I deal with Jim, I play my cards close to my chest and don't say a word till I've got five aces to open.

I shared the astonishing discovery with Millie; then we went back in the woods for eucalyptus leaves and the potting soil at the base of the trees to show Jim. "He must have come by boat," said Millie as we were filling the specimen Baggies.

" 'He'?"

"Whoever put all these things here. I think he stole Susie, too. And I'm sure it was a he."

"I could agree, but we're not ready to bring the case to court yet. So shut up and find some evidence."

She pouted at me. "Whatever happened to our decorous, Old-Worldly Whatsit and Bones act?"

I sneered. "You're lookin' at Mike Hammer, babe."

"Just call me Anvil, honey," she answered, wiggling.

"Later. At home. If it's too late for skeeters, it's probably no-see-um season."

I've never met such a lascivious creature as Millie. Nor had I realized what a horny old goat I am till I met her. If there were any mosquitoes I didn't feel them, and I thought idly afterward as we were dressing that no-see-ums don't show till the spring dry season. But the dog-gnats, till we got reclad, were a bother.

Once we were home, I called Jim. "Like to reopen the kangaroo case, tiger?"

"I never closed it. Kidnapping's a capital charge."

"Got some evidence here to astound you. It might even twitch your facial muscles."

"I don't astound easy."

"You will, buddy." This time I hung up on him for a change.

We had barely enough time for a quick shower before he showed up. Millie got my coffee and his beer ready; I lined up Exhibits A, B, C, and D on the dining table.

"This better be good. I'd be gettin' rich if I was billing mileage."

"Sit down. Take a sip, uh, guzzle. Now here's Exhibit A: eucalyptus leaves, from an otherwise native nature preserve on the southeast corner of Live Oak Key, Florida. Exhibit B, photo with eucalyptus trees marked, showing unnatural distribution. Exhibit C, manmade potting soil dug from base of same trees."

He thought a moment. "So somebody planted some trees there. It's strange, but there's a lot o' strange people here."

"Right here?"

"*Right* here. Two out o' three."

Smirking, I produced the eight by ten. "Exhibit D, enlarged detail from photograph of exotic mammal in same area."

He studied the picture. At last, ungraciously, he said, "What the hell *is* it?"

"Duck-billed platypus. Native to same part of the world as eucalyptus and Susie. They're rare, even there."

His face did move. I saw it with my own eyes.

"Well, I'll be damned," he finally mumbled.

We sat around a while theorizing. Millie even took notes on various possibility tracks. After this, we went to the scene of the crime with the chief detective—Jim was now in charge of the case, no longer a mere consultant—to show him the evidence first-hand.

On our previous trip, I'd been ready to check out Millie's hunch that the perpetrator had come by boat, till we got distracted. We now looked for a trail leading toward the water from the central glade. We found a couple that curved around and petered out, and then one that led fairly straight in what we figured was about the closest access to the sound. As we tracked down it, we saw evidence of a little machete work, a couple of human male bootprints, and one we thought—but couldn't be sure—was an old Susie-print, inbound.

We found the trail too easy to be anything but what we thought it was. It stayed to high ground, was fairly straight and free of limbs to head-height, and ended up at a kind of augmented natural boat slip where a sandy channel next to a coral-rock ledge had been deepened with some kind of shovel-and-bucket work.

"Well, we know how and what, now we gotta figure out *who*," commented Jim.

We thought about it on the way home. Afterwards, as we sat at the conference table, he finished his thought. "A stakeout could be real labor-intensive and time-consumin'. He might only come every few weeks, for all we know."

"Maybe we could have a kind of robot stakeout," put in Millie. "You know, electric eyes and infrared cameras and stuff."

"I'm not up on the state-of-the-art," I responded, "but Russ would know what's possible. My technology is limited to a black thread across the path hooked up to a box-Brownie, but there's probably something more sophisticated." We decided for me to check with Russ first, then with electronics geniuses as required and available.

Millie and Russ hadn't seen each other since he did the processing to catch the swamp rats who assaulted her and stole her car on Alligator Alley. I encouraged her to doll herself up a bit and go into the shop ahead of me.

She did. Millie has that to-the-manor-born sort of class that can support a lot of hardware without looking outré. Or that can slouch around in a pair of ragged jeans and one of my old flannel shirts and look like she's arriving at an exclusive reception. She looks quite good in the buff, too. I've never seen a nude with more *dignity* since Fine Arts 305, Advanced Life Studio.

For this occasion, she wore a simple frock in aquamarine and beige, trimmed with touches of gold and jade, mostly my gifts over the months we'd known each other. She tucked a splash of my favorite fragrance into her irresistible décolletage, and I had my hands full keeping my hands off her.

I parked a few spaces down from Color Lab and let Millie go in before I left the car. I dawdled at a couple of windows and then went into the shop. Russ barely glanced in my direction.

"Be with you in a little while, Walt," he said over his shoulder, and went back to breathing down her cleavage. He was trying to sell her a camera, a roll of film, or mostly darkroom lessons.

I let her charm him a while longer and then spoke. "I have some news for you, Russ, if you can stop drooling down that young lady's bosom for a minute." And to her: "He's married, miss."

Russ was nonplussed. This was a total violation of code. Preferable is to stand by and let your buddy score. Barely tolerable is to move in and try to share the action. Simply Not Done is to torpedo his effort.

Hardly concealing his irritation, he asked curtly, "Like what ind of news?"

"Like, do you remember the ugly prints you did of the asault victim back in July?"

He almost forgot my breach of manners, remembering the ruesome pix. "Ye-ah."

"Well, you've been trying to put the make on her for the last even minutes."

He did a doubletake, mouth agape. "Well, I'll—be—amned," he finally got out, staring at her. "You're, ah, well, I ean—"

"Thank you," she said. "*I* think I look a lot better, too."

"I take back what I said, Walt. I still think you've got lousy aste in photo equipment, but your taste in women makes up or it."

As soon as we got settled down, I started telling him what ve needed, only hinting at the why, and reassuring him that e'd get the full story soon.

"The photo stuff we can do, just for the amusement of it. 've even got some experimental polysensitive film that ought o give you a usable print day or night, though not studio qual-y under any circumstances."

"We just want to identify a face."

"I'd say fifty percent chance or better. With two cameras nd multiple exposures, better I.D. than passport or police pic-ıres. There will be some expense for renting electronic stuff, ut I can save you the deposit and set it up for you.

Next day about one, having kept a fitful watch meanwhile, im and I went to Russ for the equipment and instructions.

"The last one was better looking," said Russ, looking at Jim.

"I trust you better with this one," I retorted.

The mechanism, once organized by the experts and ex-lained to us, was simple enough. When we got home with it, ve set up an infrared eye across the trail near the boat landing. Vhen the beam was broken, it would set off two automatic ameras set at different angles. Each would shoot, advance to ıe next frame, and wait for the next trip. As a bonus, Russ's lectronics expert had wired in a short-range CB transmitter so we would get an audible signal at the cottage if we were home, otherwise we would check the film counter daily.

All the equipment was weatherproofed, and we set it up in such a way that only the CIA, if they knew it was there in the first place, could find it. Jim and I walked through the first two frames to test it, and it worked. We heard a slight buzzing click from the trail, and decided to scatter dry cabbage-palm fronds on the path at the sensor, so their crunching would mask the camera sound. That ran us up to frame four. We spent frames five and six checking the CB, and headed home.

We decided it was good policy not to actively pursue the culprit, just to monitor daily or so for film counts and tracks, and watch from the point to identify the boat if he came westward, which we considered unlikely.

We spent a couple of boring days waiting for signals that never came, or following up false signals that were either animals or some kind of radio interference. The film count went slowly up, but no one used the landing. We relaxed our obsession and went back to, for us, a normalish life.

Then one day there was an unusual total quiet: the bay was flat—you could see Shell Island reflected in it—no breeze stirring, no birds, no powerboaters. Millie was hand sewing, I was reading, Sam was asleep, and the fridge had just stopped. I was about to open my mouth to comment on it when we heard a fairsized outboard a mile or so east of the point, faintly but clearly. We both listened as the motor came in, changed pitch, idled down, sped up, and then—so far as we could tell—stopped entirely.

A couple of minutes later the radio alarm sounded. "I think this is it," Millie whispered.

"Me too," I responded as quietly. I thought of calling Jim, but decided on quiet instead. Less than an hour later the CB binged again. By now the background noise had increased, but being tuned for it, we heard the outboard race, change gears, and settle into a steady cruise, headed eastward away from us.

Counting dressing time, it took us no more than ten minutes to cover the now familiar trail. The film counters had gone up two notches, and the dry sandy part of the trail showed boot tracks about a size eleven, as close as we could tell identical to the ones we'd seen earlier. Down at the slip, a scuffle of tracks—one man only—and marks of something heavy being off-loaded. Probably a bag of Purina Wombat Chow, we figured.

We were sure we had our man, but for caution we left everything in place, removed the film, and replaced it with new rolls. We needn't have bothered.

The only reason it took thirty minutes to get to Russ's shop was that the drawbridge was up. "You're lucky this stuff uses the same chemistry," he said when we rushed in with our precious cartridges. "You get our usual one-hour service, less time off for good behavior. Come back in forty-five minutes, Walt, and meanwhile I'll show the lady how I operate in the darkroom."

"Russell!" came a voice from behind the curtain.

"Yes, dear, only joking."

We spent a couple of minutes chatting with Russ and his pretty assistant, Debbie Sue, who seemed to be Mrs. Russ or close to it, then went shopping till time for the prints to be ready.

"Got a couple of real criminal types here," he said when we returned. He handed us the prints of Jim and me. We really did look pretty rough-and-ready. "And here's some four-legged ones." There was a fierce-looking, scarred old boar I'm glad we didn't meet, and the upper half of something that *could* have been a wombat, or a fat collie, or almost anything. "But this is probably the guy you want." I think we could have recognized the character on the street from three of the four shots, two profiles and one more or less full face. He looked like the prototype for Crocodile Dundee, Aussie-type hat and all.

"Any doubts, Whatsit?"

"None atall, Bones."

"We'll bring the equipment in tomorrow, Russ. This part of the job is done." We paid him and left.

Of course we stopped at Shrimptown on the way home. If *Mary Jo* hadn't been in, I think we'd have tried to whistle her back all the way from the Campeachy Banks.

Jim actually grinned when he saw the shots of the Aussie. And even if he didn't walk the streets of Palm City and the byways of Mosby County clad in his Professional Australian uniform, we had a good face and a close approximation of size and shape, a solid six footer in good condition. "Two steps ahead of us now," said Jim. "First track him down, then do sumpin' about it."

We had two possible leads: Ed Seeger, who might have some personal acquaintance of him without suspecting him, and Nigel Nichols, a friend of mine who belonged to the local chapter of the Commonwealth Club, a loose organization of home-counties British and ex-Colonials. We got Russ to run some extra prints through in a hurry—for a price—and headed in opposite directions.

I tracked Nigel down in his office, where he occasionally dabbles in stockbrokering under the aegis of a thirty-year-old Green Card. I showed him our mug shots.

"Oh, MacKenzie," he said immediately. "What's he done now—another drunk and disorderly, public nudity, young girls?"

"We think he used a kangaroo without permission. But this is all a very private affair, not a police matter if we can help it."

"Something he might do, yes. A bit too Australian for his own good. Known amongst his intimates as Wildman, or the Dingo Jingo. Been practicing Stryne for years, though he's been known to speak the Queen's on special occasions."

"Does he have a real name?"

"Ian. His family were too wild for the Highlands, and transported themselves Down Under a couple of generations back. Decent chap, actually, if one Makes Allowances. Used to have a pet 'roo he doted on, Judy or Sally or something totally inappropriate like that."

"You've been a great help, Nigel."

I thanked him, shook his hand, and sped on my way.

Jim had learned from Ed that the guy was named Crocodile MacKenzie and represented himself as a wild animal specialist. There was only one Ian MacKenzie in the Palm City phone book; rather than put him on guard, we were going to go straight to his house, but Millie volunteered to put on her telephone solicitor act first. He was home, and the voice was right. Jim and I hopped in the car and were there within thirty minutes.

I half expected the Australian flag to be flying in front of the house, but it looked fairly normal from the outside. Jim knocked.

Standing in the doorway, he looked *mighty* big—not as tall as me, but a lot of muscle. I hoped he wasn't really all that violent.

"Mr. MacKenzie," began Jim, "we need to talk to you about wildlife conservation—'specially kangaroos and platypuses, and that kind o' thing."

MacKenzie inflated, clouded over like a Florida thunderhead, then relaxed and opened the door wider.

"Come on in. I suppose I expected this sooner or later." His accent slowly relaxed, too, and he sounded as if he'd lived here for years.

"This isn't an official visit, Mr. MacKenzie," Jim continued. "We're just tryin' to solve a problem before it gets outa hand. Did you know you nearly got Susie shot? Wildlife officer came out with a gun, this man here barely managed to save her."

Jim had just redefined us as allies, defusing MacKenzie's remaining antagonism. For a hardnosed ex-cop, he's a damn good diplomat when he decides to be. There was a long conversation, ranging from Australian government wildlife and Abo policy to who—if anyone—had clear title to Susie, who had apparently been truly his own pet kangaroo at one time and from whom he felt unfairly separated by a third party who dropped out of the picture before we ever got into it.

Jim, for all he comes on like a merciless son of a bitch, has a streak of humanity in him and some keen intuitions about people. Before the evening was far along, he'd arranged for a meeting between MacKenzie and Ed, and we firmed up the arrangements the next day.

The girls, of course, had to go, too, and we ended up taking two cars. The two principals started out guarded but civil; before the meeting was over they'd managed their zealotry and were talking big plans.

"What I had in mind for the Australian habitat," Ed was

saying as we withdrew unnoticed, "was to take that pond down yonder, build an island in the middle with a moat all around, narrow plank walkway and a drawbridge to keep the small animals from getting off the island at night . . ."

"I've a bit of capital I might consider turning into a project like that. Then of course I have some initial stock scattered about here and there . . ."

On the way back we were already looking forward to the corroboree when roundup time started in our woods.

"Just one question left," Jim broke in. "Who blew the whistle on him and nearly got Susie shot?"

We all groaned at the thought of Jim's chewing away at one more unanswered question in the Mystery of the Missing Marsupial.

"That's your project, Jim," Millie answered for all of us. "We've done our part."

It was a couple of days later that the fill-dirt truck pulled up by our driveway.

"Where do you want it dumped?" the driver asked.

"Dumped?"

"This load of manure here. Mr. Seeger said you need it for your garden."

There was at least five tons dry of the stuff, or ten tons wet, which it was. Millie's eyes lit up like it was a chest of jewels, and my whole day was suddenly clouded with dread. I turned around and walked into the cottage, knowing she'd tell him to put it east of the garden patch, which would put it upwind of us for the rest of the dry season.

Which she did. And it was.

GROUNDHOG

BENNIE LEE SINCLAIR

"Here comes Sally with a snicker and a grin,
Groundhog grease all over her chin—Groundhog!"
                              —Southern Appalachian folk song

Pumpkin Creek cut across the bottom fields in a straight line but went underground several times for stretches of a dozen yards or so. There was a place where farm equipment was able to safely pass over these underground channels, a clearly marked crossing, making it even more puzzling how the boys' truck came to rest upside down in the creek. Even then, it might not have been a disaster if they hadn't been drunk and going so fast, night-hunting and joyriding over the rough turf.

It was the preacher's grown but slow son Ladson who found them. When he looked down from the parsonage window about daylight, there stood the red truck with its wheels in the air, and he at least knew enough to know it was wrong, and woke his mother. Soon there were a half-dozen men standing knee-deep in creek water straining to see through the shattered cab windows the dead boys, Johnny Bledsoe and his little brother Tommy, and redheaded Billy Hatcher, who was still alive, but they didn't know it yet.

Billy Hatcher was still living because of the buffer the steering wheel made, but though that was certainly lucky, it made him guilty, too, of driving too fast and trespassing drunk where he shouldn't have been, in Roy Ashton's truck, which he hadn't even bothered to borrow.

The Bledsoe boys' parents vowed never to forgive Billy Hatcher, and as bad feeling spread, families and friends were split apart taking sides, those who thought Billy ought to go to jail, and those who thought he was too young to be responsible. It depended on how you viewed sixteen.

I didn't know all this at first, when I bought the bottom fields and moved into Pumpkin Valley—only that there was division and I would be expected to take sides eventually. I was newly widowed, and wanted only to find peace and hope. It was in all innocence that I let Billy Hatcher, by then eighteen, come to work for me—and Betty Bledsoe, the dead boys' mother, drive for me. I knew she had suffered a tragedy, but I didn't know what, and I knew Billy Hatcher wasn't well liked, but I didn't know why. I sensed there was something explosive waiting to happen in our valley, but I certainly didn't expect to fuel it.

The trouble began because I was fond of the groundhogs and I didn't want anybody to kill them. It pained me to see them in the roadside stands, stuffed as souvenirs, wearing doll sunglasses and little baseball caps. I figured we farmers planted enough to share a little, and now that I owned the bottoms I kept a gate up to keep people out. But boys still slipped down there to shoot at the groundhogs—often just for target practice. Nobody seemed to eat the meat anymore. I resented the killing and determined to put a stop to it. But with the first No Hunting sign I made enemies. Some of my neighbors grew silent, and some of the mothers came at me like bantam hens protecting the rights of their dibs. "My Kenny's been hunting down there all his life," they'd say, or, "My Chad don't bother nobody by huntin' down there."

"It bothers *me*," I'd say, "and it certainly bothers the groundhogs!"

Betty Bledsoe, surprisingly, took my side, taking up the cause of the groundhogs. "I hate to hear all the shooting and noise down there," she confided. "That place ought to be left in peace." This she said while driving me to church, prim in her habitual colors, red, white, and blue.

Granny Endower, our guest in the backseat, observed, slowly and meaningfully, "Groundhogs ain't got souls. What does it matter?"

"God instructed Noah to take the animals into his care," I countered. "That's what I'm doing."

On the way home, once Granny Endower had been let out, Betty Bledsoe, between slow tears, told me about her boys.

So when Billy Hatcher came to me later that week asking permission to go nights to the bottom fields—he didn't want to hunt, he said, he just wanted to sit and think and listen to the night sounds—I acquiesced. I thought I understood. It was the place of his guilt, and he needed to come to terms with it. "Of course," I said, with empathy.

Now and then I heard a blast or a blam and figured the groundhogs' ranks were being depleted by some quick trespasser, but not often. It was frustrating knowing I couldn't get down there quickly enough to catch anyone, living up the mountain above the parsonage as I did, and I could no longer depend on Ladson to keep an eye out, he having been sent away to an institution. But most of the boys seemed to stay away, and whenever I passed the field two or three of the funny furry groundhogs always sat up from their foraging like alert sentries. I heard an occasional rumor that someone was setting traps for them, but I had no proof.

Billy Hatcher with his red hair and special guilt was the only one I permitted to go down there, and, in a quiet moment, I told Betty Bledsoe about his request and my reasoning.

My comments seemed to make an impression. Betty was— or had been—a mother. Now she had no sons to fuss over. Billy, perhaps because he had so few friends, seemed to be maturing into a responsible if reticent young man. He looked, to me, like an angel ordained against his will, with his fiery red hair and his quick temper suppressed now by determined quiet words and attention to whatever he considered duty.

I'd heard he had never known much love in his upbringing, and I began to fantasize that he and Betty would between them form some shared bond from their tragedy. It would help assuage his guilt, and her now childless loneliness. And so I was pleased when Betty began coming by afternoons while Billy was still there. That first time she nodded at him, the merest of greetings, I felt my heart lift in a way it had not lifted for years. I almost felt I could believe in peace and hope again, in happy endings. When I saw Billy striking out across the bottoms in late summer, groundhogs making an occasional dark shadow on the stubble before him, and Betty, parked in her car at sunset, looking out and down at that place where her sons drew their last breaths, I felt overjoyed that I'd helped ease the terrible tension between them.

Not many nights after, the explosion of a double-barreled shotgun woke me. It was the close of an Indian summer night, a faint rosy hue was beginning to lift the darkness, and only my thudding heart spoke of terror. Then *Blam! Blam!* the gun sounded again, too close. The bottoms? I covered my head with the pillow and must have dozed. I woke to a sound even more unfamiliar to our valley—that of a siren.

I got up, put on a warm robe and my glasses, and went out on the porch. I could see a flashing light below the parsonage. Then the EMS ambulance started up, returning to town—but slowly, without the siren. I watched it cross the gap. Another siren approached—the deputy's car? I thought about dressing, going down to the bottoms to see what had happened, but I knew that Granny Endower would call me soon enough with the news.

Until then, I went into the kitchen to make some coffee, and I was there when Betty Bledsoe knocked at the front door. I might not have recognized her, but for the familiar red, white, and blue she wore. She stood there, disheveled, a stranger in her swaying stance, with the gun and heavy towsack she carried. Blood dripped from it onto the porch floor that Billy had painted and kept so carefully clean for me.

"There's groundhogs in here!" Betty's eyes and face blazed. She must have run all the way from the bottoms carrying the heavy dripping sack, she was so winded and red. "Do you understand me?" she pleaded. *"Groundhogs!"*

I looked at her uncomprehendingly.

"That's all he was doing, all he was going to the bottoms for, all that time . . . trapping the groundhogs!"

"Who?" I asked weakly.

"Billy Hatcher! One of the traps was right there where the truck went in, where my boys . . . There was a groundhog caught, chewing its foot off, when along he comes, checking the traps, whistling . . ."

She handed me the sack. I staggered back from the weight, blood dripping now inside my clean house.

"The ambulance?" I asked dully.

"So I shot him. I killed him! What else could I do?" She threw up her hands wildly. "He was killing the groundhogs!"

DEATH AT THE EXCELSIOR

P. G. WODEHOUSE

The room was the typical bedroom of the typical boarding-house, furnished, insofar as it could be said to be furnished at all, with a severe simplicity. It contained two beds, a pine chest of drawers, a strip of faded carpet, and a wash basin. But there was that on the floor which set this room apart from a thousand rooms of the same kind. Flat on his back, with his hands tightly clenched and one leg twisted oddly under him and with his teeth gleaming through his gray beard in a horrible grin, Captain John Gunner stared up at the ceiling with eyes that saw nothing.

Until a moment before, he had had the little room all to himself. But now two people were standing just inside the door, looking down at him. One was a large policeman, who twisted his helmet nervously in his hands. The other was a tall gaunt old woman in a rusty black dress, who gazed with pale eyes at the dead man. Her face was quite expressionless.

The woman was Mrs. Pickett, owner of the Excelsior boarding-house. The policeman's name was Grogan. He was a genial giant, a terror to the riotous element of the waterfront, but obviously ill at ease in the presence of death. He drew in his breath, wiped his forehead, and whispered, "Look at his eyes, ma'am!"

Mrs. Pickett had not spoken a word since she had brought the policeman into the room, and she did not do so now. Constable Grogan looked at her quickly. He was afraid of Mother Pickett, as was everybody else along the waterfront. Her silence, her pale eyes, and the quiet decisiveness of her personality cowed even the tough old salts who patronized the Excelsior. She was a formidable influence in that little community of sailormen.

"That's just how I found him," said Mrs. Pickett. She did not speak loudly, but her voice made the policeman start.

He wiped his forehead again. "It might have been apoplexy," he hazarded.

Mrs. Pickett said nothing. There was a sound of footsteps outside, and a young man entered, carrying a black bag.

"Good morning, Mrs. Pickett. I was told that—good Lord!" The young doctor dropped to his knees beside the body and raised one of the arms. After a moment he lowered it gently to the floor and shook his head in grim resignation.

"He's been dead for hours," he announced. "When did you find him?"

"Twenty minutes back," replied the old woman. "I guess he died last night. He never would be called in the morning. Said he liked to sleep on. Well, he's got his wish."

"What did he die of, sir?" asked the policeman.

"It's impossible to say without an examination," the doctor answered. "It looks like a stroke, but I'm pretty sure it isn't. It might be a coronary attack, but I happen to know his blood pressure was normal, and his heart sound. He called in to see me only a week ago and I examined him thoroughly. But sometimes you can be deceived. The inquest will tell us."

He eyed the body almost resentfully. "I can't understand it. The man had no right to drop dead like this. He was a tough old sailor who ought to have been good for another twenty years. If you want my honest opinion—though I can't possibly be certain until after the inquest—I should say he had been poisoned."

"How would he be poisoned?" asked Mrs. Pickett quietly.

"That's more than I can tell you. There's no glass about that he could have drunk it from. He might have got it in capsule form. But why should he have done it? He was always a pretty cheerful sort of man, wasn't he?"

"Yes, sir," said the constable. "He had the name of being a joker in these parts. Kind of sarcastic, they tell me, though he never tried it on me."

"He must have died quite early last night," said the doctor. He turned to Mrs. Pickett. "What's become of Captain Muller? If he shares this room he ought to be able to tell us something."

"Captain Muller spent the night with some friends at Portsmouth," said Mrs. Pickett. "He left right after supper, and hasn't returned."

The doctor stared thoughtfully about the room, frowning.

"I don't like it. I can't understand it. If this had happened in India I should have said the man had died from some form of snake bite. I was out there two years, and I've seen a hundred cases of it. The poor devils all looked just like this. But the thing's ridiculous. How could a man be bitten by a snake in a Southampton waterfront boardinghouse? Was the door locked when you found him, Mrs. Pickett?"

Mrs. Pickett nodded. "I opened it with my own key. I had been calling him and he didn't answer, so I guessed something was wrong."

The constable spoke, "You ain't touched anything, ma'am? They're always very particular about that. If the doctor's right and there's been anything up, that's the first thing they'll ask."

"Everything's just as I found it."

"What's that on the floor beside him?" the doctor asked.

"Only his harmonica. He liked to play it of an evening in his room. I've had some complaints about it from some of the gentlemen, but I never saw any harm, so long as he didn't play it too late."

"Seems as if he was playing it when—it happened," Constable Grogan said. "That don't look much like suicide, sir."

"I didn't say it was suicide."

Grogan whistled. "You don't think—"

"I'm not thinking anything—until after the inquest. All I say is that it's queer."

Another aspect of the matter seemed to strike the policeman. "I guess this ain't going to do the Excelsior any good, ma'am," he said sympathetically.

Mrs. Pickett shrugged.

"I suppose I had better go and notify the coroner," said the doctor.

He went out, and after a momentary pause the policeman followed. Constable Grogan was not greatly troubled with nerves, but he felt a decided desire to be where he could not see the dead man's staring eyes.

Mrs. Pickett remained where she was, looking down at the still form on the floor. Her face was expressionless, but inwardly she was tormented and alarmed. It was the first time such a thing as this had happened at the Excelsior, and, as Constable Grogan had suggested, it was not likely to increase the attractiveness of the house in the eyes of possible boarders. It was not the threatened pecuniary loss which was troubling her. As far as money was concerned, she could have lived comfortably on her savings, for she was richer than most of her friends supposed. It was the blot on the escutcheon of the Excelsior, the stain on its reputation, which was tormenting her.

The Excelsior was her life. Starting many years before, beyond the memory of the oldest boarder, she had built up a model establishment. Men spoke of it as a place where you were fed well, cleanly housed, and where petty robbery was unknown.

Such was the chorus of praise that it is not likely that much harm could come to the Excelsior from a single mysterious death, but Mother Pickett was not consoling herself with that.

She looked at the dead man with pale grim eyes. Out in the hallway the doctor's voice further increased her despair. He was talking to the police on the telephone, and she could distinctly hear his every word.

The offices of Mr. Paul Snyder's Detective Agency in New Oxford Street had grown in the course of a dozen years from a single room to an impressive suite bright with polished wood, clicking typewriters, and other evidences of success. Where once Mr. Snyder had sat and waited for clients and attended to them himself, he now sat in his private office and directed eight assistants.

He had just accepted a case—a case that might be nothing at all or something exceedingly big. It was on the latter possibility that he had gambled. The fee offered was, judged by his present standards of prosperity, small. But the bizarre facts, coupled with something in the personality of the client, had won him over. He briskly touched the bell and requested that Mr. Oakes should be sent in to him.

Elliott Oakes was a young man who both amused and interested Mr. Snyder, for though he had only recently joined the staff, he made no secret of his intention of revolutionizing the methods of the agency. Mr. Snyder himself, in common with most of his assistants, relied for results on hard work and common sense. He had never been a detective of the showy type. Results had justified his methods, but he was perfectly aware that young Mr. Oakes looked on him as a dull old man who had been miraculously favored by luck.

Mr. Snyder had selected Oakes for the case in hand principally because it was one where inexperience could do no harm, and where the brilliant guesswork which Oakes preferred to call his inductive reasoning might achieve an unexpected success.

Another motive actuated Mr. Snyder. He had a strong suspicion that the conduct of this case was going to have the beneficial result of lowering Oakes's self-esteem. If failure achieved this end, Mr. Snyder felt that failure, though it would not help the agency, would not be an unmixed ill.

The door opened and Oakes entered tensely. He did everything tensely, partly from a natural nervous energy, and partly as a pose. He was a lean young man, with dark eyes and a thin-lipped mouth, and he looked quite as much like a typical detective as Mr. Snyder looked like a comfortable and prosperous stockbrocker.

"Sit down, Oakes," said Mr. Snyder. "I've got a job for you."

Oakes sank into a chair like a crouching leopard and placed the tips of his fingers together. He nodded curtly. It was part of his pose to be keen and silent.

"I want you to go to this address"—Mr. Snyder handed him an envelope—"and look around. The address is of a sailors' boardinghouse down in Southampton. You know the sort of place—retired sea captains and so on live there. All most respectable. In all its history nothing more sensational has ever happened than a case of suspected cheating at halfpenny nap. Well, a man has died there."

"Murdered?" Oakes asked.

"I don't know. That's for you to find out. The coroner left it open. 'Death by Misadventure' was the verdict, and I don't blame him. I don't see how it could have been murder. The door was locked on the inside, so nobody could have got in."

"The window?"

"The window was open, granted. But the room is on the second floor. Anyway, you may dismiss the window. I remember that old lady saying there were bars across it, and that nobody could have squeezed through."

Oakes's eyes glistened. "What was the cause of death?" he asked.

Mr. Snyder coughed. "Snake bite," he said.

Oakes's careful calm deserted him. He uttered a cry of astonishment. "Why, that's incredible!"

"It's the literal truth. The medical examination proved that the fellow had been killed by snake poison—cobra, to be exact, which is found principally in India."

"Cobra!"

"Just so. In a Southampton boardinghouse, in a room with a door locked on the inside, this man was stung by a cobra. To add a little mystification to the limpid simplicity of the affair, when the door was opened there was no sign of any cobra. It couldn't have got out through the door, because the door was locked. It couldn't have got out the window, because the window was too high up, and snakes can't jump. And it couldn't have got up the chimney, because there was no chimney. So there you have it."

He looked at Oakes with a certain quiet satisfaction. It had come to his ears that Oakes had been heard to complain of the infantile nature of the last two cases to which he had been assigned. He had even said that he hoped some day to be given a problem which should be beyond the reasoning powers of a child of six. It seemed to Mr. Snyder that Oakes was about to get his wish.

"I should like further details," said Oakes, a little breathlessly.

"You had better apply to Mrs. Pickett, who owns the boardinghouse," Mr. Snyder said. "It was she who put the case in my hands. She is convinced that it is murder. But if we exclude ghosts, I don't see how any third party could have taken a hand in the thing at all. However, she wanted a man from this agency, and was prepared to pay for him, so I promised her I would send one. It is not our policy to turn business away."

He smiled wryly. "In pursuance of that policy I want you to go and put up at Mrs. Pickett's boardinghouse and do your best to enhance the reputation of our agency. I would suggest that you pose as a ship's chandler or something of that sort. You will have to be something maritime or they'll be suspicious of you. And if your visit produces no other results, it will, at least, enable you to make the acquaintance of a very remarkable woman. I commend Mrs. Pickett to your notice. By the way, she says she will help you in your investigations."

Oakes laughed shortly. The idea amused him.

"It's a mistake to scoff at amateur assistance, my boy," said Mr. Snyder in the benevolently paternal manner which had made a score of criminals refuse to believe him a detective until the moment when the handcuffs snapped on their wrists. "Crime investigation isn't an exact science. Success or failure depends in a large measure on applied common sense and the possession of a great deal of special information. Mrs. Pickett knows certain things which neither you nor I know, and it's just possible that she may have some stray piece of information which will provide the key to the entire mystery."

Oakes laughed again. "It is very kind of Mrs. Pickett," he said, "but I prefer to trust to my own methods." Oakes rose, his face purposeful. "I'd better be starting at once," he said. "I'll send you reports from time to time."

"Good. The more detailed the better," said Mr. Snyder genially. "I hope your visit to the Excelsior will be pleasant. And cultivate Mrs. Pickett. She's worthwhile."

The door closed, and Mr. Snyder lighted a fresh cigar. Dashed young fool, he thought and turned his mind to other matters.

*   *   *

A day later Mr. Snyder sat in his office reading a typewritten report. It appeared to be of a humorous nature, for, as he read, chuckles escaped him. Finishing the last sheet he threw his head back and laughed heartily. The manuscript had not been intended by its author for humorous effect. What Mr. Snyder had been reading was the first of Elliott Oakes's reports from the Excelsior. It read as follows:

"I am sorry to be unable to report any real progress. I have formed several theories which I will put forward later, but at present I cannot say that I am hopeful.

"Directly I arrived I sought out Mrs. Pickett, explained who I was, and requested her to furnish me with any further information which might be of service to me. She is a strange silent woman, who impressed me as having very little intelligence. Your suggestion that I should avail myself of her assistance seems more curious than ever, now that I have seen her.

"The whole affair seems to me at the moment of writing quite inexplicable. Assuming that this Captain Gunner was murdered there appears to have been no motive for the crime whatsoever. I have made careful inquiries about him, and find that he was a man of 55; had spent nearly 40 years of his life at sea, the last dozen in command of his own ship; was of a somewhat overbearing disposition, though with a fund of rough humour; he had travelled all over the world, and had been a resident of the Excelsior for about ten months. He had a small annuity, and no other money at all, which disposes of money as the motive for the crime.

"In my character of James Burton, a retired ship's chandler, I have mixed with the other boarders, and have heard all they have to say about the affair. I gather that the deceased was by no means popular. He appears to have had a bitter tongue, and I have not met one man who seems to regret his death. On the other hand, I have heard nothing which would suggest that he had any active and violent enemies. He was simply the unpopular boarder—there is always one in every boardinghouse—but nothing more.

"I have seen a good deal of the man who shared his room—another sea captain named Muller. He is a big silent person, and it is not easy to get him to talk. As regards the death of

Captain Gunner he can tell me nothing. It seems that on the night of the tragedy he was away at Portsmouth with some friends. All I have got from him is some information as to Captain Gunner's habits, which leads nowhere.

"The dead man seldom drank, except at night when he would take some whisky. His head was not strong, and a little of the spirit was enough to make him semi-intoxicated, when he would be hilarious and often insulting. I gather that Muller found him a difficult roommate, but he is one of those placid persons who can put up with anything. He and Gunner were in the habit of playing draughts together every night in their room, and Gunner had a harmonica which he played frequently. Apparently he was playing it very soon before he died, which is significant, as seeming to dispose of any idea of suicide.

"As I say, I have one or two theories, but they are in a very nebulous state. The most plausible is that on one of his visits to India—I have ascertained that he made several voyages there—Captain Gunner may in some way have fallen foul of the natives. The fact that he certainly died of the poison of an Indian snake supports this theory. I am making inquiries as to the movements of several Indian sailors who were here in their ships at the time of the tragedy.

"I have another theory. Does Mrs. Pickett know more about this affair than she appears to? I may be wrong in my estimate of her mental qualities. Her apparent stupidity may be cunning. But here again, the absence of motive brings me up against a dead wall. I must confess that at present I do not see my way clearly. However, I will write again shortly."

Mr. Snyder derived the utmost enjoyment from the report. He liked the substance of it, and above all, he was tickled by the bitter tone of frustration which characterized it. Oakes was baffled, and his knowledge of Oakes told him that the sensation of being baffled was gall and wormwood to that high-spirited young man. Whatever might be the result of this investigation, it would teach him the virtue of patience.

He wrote his assistant a short note:

Dear Oakes,

Your report received. You certainly seem to have got
the hard case which, I hear, you were pining for. Don't
build too much on plausible motives in a case of this
sort. Fauntleroy, the London murderer, killed a woman
for no other reason than that she had thick ankles.
Many years ago I myself was on a case where a man
murdered an intimate friend because of a dispute
about a bet. My experience is that five murderers out
of ten act on the whim of the moment, without anything
which, properly speaking, you could call a motive at all.

Yours very cordially,
Paul Snyder

P.S. I don't think much of your Pickett theory. However, you're in charge. I wish you luck.

Young Mr. Oakes was not enjoying himself. For the first
time in his life the self-confidence which characterized all his
actions seemed to be failing him. The change had taken place
almost overnight. The fact that the case had the appearance of
presenting the unusual had merely stimulated him at first. But
then doubts had crept in and the problem had begun to appear
insoluble.

True, he had only just taken it up, but something told him
that, for all the progress he was likely to make, he might just
as well have been working on it steadily for a month. He was
completely baffled. And every moment which he spent in the
Excelsior boardinghouse made it clearer to him that that infer-
nal old woman with the pale eyes thought him an incompetent
fool. It was that, more than anything, which made him acutely
conscious of his lack of success. His nerves were being sorely
troubled by the quiet scorn of Mrs. Pickett's gaze. He began to
think that perhaps he had been a shade too self-confident and
abrupt in the short interview which he had had with her on his
arrival.

As might have been expected, his first act, after his brief interview with Mrs. Pickett, was to examine the room where the
tragedy had taken place. The body was gone, but otherwise
nothing had been moved.

Oakes belonged to the magnifying-glass school of detection. The first thing he did on entering the room was to make a careful examination of the floor, the walls, the furniture, and the window sill. He would have hotly denied the assertion that he did this because it looked well, but he would have been hard put to it to advance any other reason.

If he discovered anything, his discoveries were entirely negative and served only to deepen the mystery. As Mr. Snyder had said, there was no chimney, and nobody could have entered through the locked door.

There remained the window. It was small, and apprehensiveness, perhaps, of the possibility of burglars had caused the proprietress to make it doubly secure with two iron bars. No human being could have squeezed his way through.

It was late that night that he wrote and dispatched to headquarters the report which had amused Mr. Snyder.

Two days later Mr. Snyder sat at his desk, staring with wide unbelieving eyes at a telegram he had just received. It read as follows:

HAVE SOLVED GUNNER MYSTERY. RETURNING. OAKES.

Mr. Snyder narrowed his eyes and rang the bell.

"Send Mr. Oakes to me directly he arrives," he said.

He was pained to find that his chief emotion was one of bitter annoyance. The swift solution of such an apparently insoluble problem would reflect the highest credit of the agency, and there were picturesque circumstances connected with the case which would make it popular with the newspapers and lead to its being given a great deal of publicity.

Yet, in spite of all this, Mr. Snyder was annoyed. He realized now how large a part the desire to reduce Oakes's self-esteem had played with him. He further realized, looking at the thing honestly, that he had been firmly convinced that the young man would not come within a mile of a reasonable solution of the mystery. He had desired only that his failure would prove a valuable educational experience for him. For he believed that failure at this particular point in his career would make Oakes a more valuable asset to the agency.

But now here Oakes was, within a ridiculously short space of time, returning to the fold, not humble and defeated, but triumphant. Mr. Snyder looked forward with apprehension to the young man's probable demeanor under the intoxicating influence of victory.

His apprehensions were well grounded. He had barely finished the third of the series of cigars which, like milestones, marked the progress of his afternoon, when the door opened and young Oakes entered. Mr. Snyder could not repress a faint moan at the sight of him. One glance was enough to tell him that his worst fears were realized.

"I got your telegram," said Mr. Snyder.

Oakes nodded. "It surprised you, eh?" he asked.

Mr. Snyder resented the patronizing tone of the question, but he had resigned himself to be patronized, and keep his anger in check.

"Yes," he replied, "I must say it did surprise me. I didn't gather from your report that you had even found a clue. Was it the Indian theory that turned the trick?"

Oakes laughed tolerantly. "Oh, I never really believed that preposterous theory for one moment. I just put it in to round out my report. I hadn't begun to think about the case then—not really think."

Mr. Snyder, nearly exploding with wrath, extended his cigar case. "Light up and tell me all about it," he said, controlling his anger.

"Well, I won't say I haven't earned this," said Oakes, puffing away. He let the ash of his cigar fall delicately to the floor—another action which seemed significant to his employer. As a rule his assistants, unless particularly pleased with themselves, used the ashtray.

"My first act on arriving," Oakes said, "was to have a talk with Mrs. Pickett. A very dull old woman."

"Curious. She struck me as rather intelligent."

"Not on your life. She gave me no assistance whatever. I then examined the room where the death had taken place. It was exactly as you described it. There was no chimney, the door had been locked on the inside, and the one window was too high up. At first sight it looked extremely unpromising.

Then I had a chat with some of the other boarders. They had nothing of any importance to contribute. Most of them simply gibbered. I then gave up trying to get help from the outside and resolved to rely on my own intelligence."

He smiled triumphantly. "It is a theory of mine, Mr. Snyder, which I have found valuable that, in nine cases out of ten, remarkable things don't happen."

"I don't quite follow you there," Mr. Snyder interrupted.

"I will put it another way, if you like. What I mean is that the simplest explanation is nearly always the right one. Consider this case. It seemed impossible that there should have been any reasonable explanation of the man's death. Most men would have worn themselves out guessing at wild theories. If I had started to do that, I should have been guessing now. As it is—here I am. I trusted to my belief that nothing remarkable ever happens, and I won out."

Mr. Snyder sighed softly. Oakes was entitled to a certain amount of gloating, but there could be no doubt that his way of telling a story was downright infuriating.

"I believe in the logical sequence of events. I refuse to accept effects unless they are preceded by causes. In other words, with all due respect to your possibly contrary opinions, Mr. Snyder, I simply decline to believe in a murder unless there was a motive for it. The first thing I set myself to ascertain was—what was the motive for the murder of Captain Gunner? And after thinking it over and making every possible inquiry, I decided that there was no motive. Therefore, there was no murder."

Mr. Snyder's mouth opened, and he obviously was about to protest. But he appeared to think better of it and Oakes proceeded: "I then tested the suicide theory. What motive was there for suicide? There was no motive. Therefore, there was no suicide."

This time Mr. Snyder spoke. "You haven't been spending the last few days in the wrong house by any chance, have you? You will be telling me next that there wasn't any dead man."

Oakes smiled. "Not at all. Captain John Gunner was dead, all right. As the medical evidence proved, he died of the bite of a cobra. It was a small cobra which came from Java."

Mr. Snyder stared at him. "How do you know?"

"I do know, beyond any possibility of doubt."

"Did you see the snake?"

Oakes shook his head.

"Then, how in heaven's name—"

"I have enough evidence to make a jury convict Mr. Snake without leaving the box."

"Then suppose you tell me this. How did your cobra from Java get out of the room?"

"By the window," replied Oakes impassively.

"How can you possibly explain that? You say yourself that the window was too high up."

"Nevertheless, it got out by the window. The logical sequence of events is proof enough that it was in the room. It killed Captain Gunner there and left traces of its presence outside. Therefore, as the window was the only exit, it must have escaped by that route. Somehow it got out of that window."

"What do you mean—it left traces of its presence outside?"

"It killed a dog in the back yard behind the house," Oakes said. "The window of Captain Gunner's room projects out over it. It is full of boxes and litter and there are a few stunted shrubs scattered about. In fact, there is enough cover to hide any small object like the body of a dog. That's why it was not discovered at first. The maid at the Excelsior came on it the morning after I sent you my report while she was emptying a box of ashes in the yard. It was just an ordinary stray dog without collar or license. The analyst examined the body and found that the dog had died of the bite of a cobra."

"But you didn't find the snake?"

"No. We cleaned out the yard till you could have eaten your breakfast there, but the snake had gone. It must have escaped through the door of the yard, which was standing ajar. That was a couple of days ago, and there has been no further tragedy. In all likelihood it is dead. The nights are pretty cold now, and it would probably have died of exposure."

"But I just don't understand how a cobra got to Southampton," said the amazed Mr. Snyder.

"Can't you guess it? I told you it came from Java."

"How did you know it did?"

"Captain Muller told me. Not directly, but I pieced it together from what he said. It seems that an old shipmate of Captain Gunner's was living in Java. They corresponded, and occasionally this man would send the captain a present as a mark of his esteem. The last present he sent was a crate of bananas. Unfortunately, the snake must have got in unnoticed. That's why I told you the cobra was a small one. Well, that's my case against Mr. Snake, and short of catching him with the goods, I don't see how I could have made out a stronger one. Don't you agree?"

It went against the grain for Mr. Snyder to acknowledge defeat, but he was a fair-minded man, and he was forced to admit that Oakes did certainly seem to have solved the impossible.

"I congratulate you, my boy," he said as heartily as he could. "To be completely frank, when you started out, I didn't think you could do it. By the way, I suppose Mrs. Pickett was pleased?"

"If she was, she didn't show it. I'm pretty well convinced she hasn't enough sense to be pleased at anything. However, she has invited me to dinner with her tonight. I imagine she'll be as boring as usual, but she made such a point of it, I had to accept."

For some time after Oakes had gone, Mr. Snyder sat smoking and thinking, in embittered meditation. Suddenly there was brought the card of Mrs. Pickett, who would be grateful if he could spare her a few moments. Mr. Snyder was glad to see Mrs. Pickett. He was a student of character, and she had interested him at their first meeting. There was something about her which had seemed to him unique, and he welcomed this second chance of studying her at close range.

She came in and sat down stiffly, balancing herself on the extreme edge of the chair in which a short while before young Oakes had lounged so luxuriously.

"How are you, Mrs. Pickett?" said Mr. Snyder genially. "I'm very glad that you could find time to pay me a visit. Well, so it wasn't murder after all."

"Sir?"

"I've been talking to Mr. Oakes, whom you met as James Burton," said the detective. "He has told me all about it."

"He told *me* all about it," said Mrs. Pickett dryly.

Mr. Snyder looked at her inquiringly. Her manner seemed more suggestive than her words.

"A conceited, headstrong young fool," said Mrs. Pickett.

It was no new picture of his assistant that she had drawn. Mr. Snyder had often drawn it himself, but at the present juncture it surprised him. Oakes, in his hour of triumph, surely did not deserve this sweeping condemnation.

"Did not Mr. Oakes's solution of the mystery satisfy you, Mrs. Pickett?"

"No."

"It struck me as logical and convincing," Mr. Snyder said.

"You may call it all the fancy names you please, Mr. Snyder. But Mr. Oakes's solution was not the right one."

"Have you an alternative to offer?"

Mrs. Pickett tightened her lips.

"If you have, I should like to hear it."

"You will—at the proper time."

"What makes you so certain that Mr. Oakes is wrong?"

"He starts out with an impossible explanation and rests his whole case on it. There couldn't have been a snake in that room because it couldn't have gotten out. The window was too high."

"But surely the evidence of the dead dog?"

Mrs. Pickett looked at him as if he had disappointed her. "I had always heard *you* spoken of as a man with common sense, Mr. Snyder."

"I have always tried to use common sense."

"Then why are you trying now to make yourself believe that something happened which could not possibly have happened just because it fits in with something which isn't easy to explain?"

"You mean that there is another explanation of the dead dog?" Mr. Snyder asked.

"Not *another*. What Mr. Oakes takes for granted is not an explanation. But there is a common-sense explanation, and if

he had not been so headstrong and conceited he might hav
found it."

"You speak as if you had found it," said Mr. Snyder.

"I have." Mrs. Pickett leaned forward as she spoke, an
stared at him defiantly.

Mr. Snyder started. "*You* have?"

"Yes."

"What is it?"

"You will know before tomorrow. In the meantime try an
think it out for yourself. A successful and prosperous detectiv
agency like yours, Mr. Snyder, ought to do something in re
turn for a fee."

There was something in her manner so reminiscent of th
school-teacher reprimanding a recalcitrant pupil that Mr. Sny
der's sense of humor came to his rescue. "We do our bes
Mrs. Pickett," he said. "But you mustn't forget that we ar
only human and cannot guarantee results."

Mrs. Pickett did not pursue the subject. Instead, she pro
ceeded to astonish Mr. Snyder by asking him to swear out
warrant for the arrest of a man known to them both on
charge of murder.

Mr. Snyder's breath was not often taken away in his ow
office. As a rule he received his clients' communication
calmly, strange as they often were. But at her words h
gasped. The thought crossed his mind that Mrs. Pickett mig
be mentally unbalanced.

Mrs. Pickett was regarding him with an unfaltering stare. T
all outward appearances she was the opposite of unbalanced.

"But you can't swear out a warrant without evidence," h
told her.

"I have evidence," she replied firmly.

"Precisely what kind of evidence?" he demanded.

"If I told you now you would think that I was out of m
mind."

"But, Mrs. Pickett, do you realize what you are asking m
to do?" I cannot make this agency responsible for the arbitrar
arrest of a man on the strength of a single individual's suspi
cions. It might ruin me. At the least it would make me a laugh
ingstock."

"Mr. Snyder, you may use your own judgment whether or
ot to swear out that warrant. You will listen to what I have to
y, and you will see for yourself how the crime was commit-
d. If after that you feel that you cannot make the arrest I will
cept your decision. I know who killed Captain Gunner," she
id. "I knew it from the beginning. But I had no proof. Now
ings have come to light and everything is clear."

Against his judgment Mr. Snyder was impressed. This
oman had the magnetism which makes for persuasiveness.

"It—it sounds incredible." Even as he spoke, he remem-
red that it had long been a professional maxim of his that
thing was incredible, and he weakened still further.

"Mr. Snyder, I ask you to swear out that warrant."

The detective gave in. "Very well," he said.

Mrs. Pickett rose. "If you will come and dine at my house
night I think I can prove to you that it will be needed. Will
u come?"

"I'll come," promised Mr. Snyder.

Mr. Snyder arrived at the Excelsior and shortly after he was
own into the little private sitting room where he found
akes, the third guest of the evening unexpectedly arrived.

Mr. Snyder looked curiously at the newcomer. Captain
uller had a peculiar fascination for him. It was not Mr. Sny-
r's habit to trust overmuch to appearances. But he could not
lp admitting that there was something about this man's as-
ct, something odd—an unnatural aspect of gloom. He bore
mself like one carrying a heavy burden. His eyes were dull,
s face haggard. The next moment the detective was re-
oaching himself with allowing his imagination to run away
ith his calmer judgment.

The door opened and Mrs. Pickett came in. She made no
ology for her lateness.

To Mr. Snyder one of the most remarkable points about the
nner was the peculiar metamorphosis of Mrs. Pickett from
e brooding silent woman he had known to the gracious and
nsiderate hostess.

Oakes appeared also to be overcome with surprise, so much
that he was unable to keep his astonishment to himself. He

had come prepared to endure a dull evening absorbed in gri
silence, and he found himself instead opposite a bottle o
champagne of a brand and year which commanded his utmo
respect. What was even more incredible, his hostess had tran
formed herself into a pleasant old lady whose only ai
seemed to be to make him feel at home.

Beside each of the guest's plates was a neat paper parce
Oakes picked his up, and stared at it in wonderment. "Wh
this is more than a party souvenir, Mrs. Pickett," he said. "It
the kind of mechanical marvel I've always wanted to have o
my desk."

"I'm glad you like it, Mr. Oakes," Mrs. Pickett said, smi
ing. "You must not think of me simply as a tired old woma
whom age has completely defeated. I am an ambitious hostes
When I give these little parties, I like to make them a succes
I want each of you to remember this dinner."

"I'm sure I will."

Mrs. Pickett smiled again. "I think you all will. You, M
Snyder." She paused. "And you, Captain Muller."

To Mr. Snyder there was so much meaning in her voice a
she said this that he was amazed that it conveyed no warnir
to Muller. Captain Muller, however, was already drinkin
heavily. He looked up when addressed and uttered a soun
which might have been taken for an expression of polite ac
quiescence. Then he filled his glass again.

Mr. Snyder's parcel revealed a watch charm fashioned i
the shape of a tiny candid-eye camera. "That," said Mrs. Pick
ett, "is a compliment to your profession." She leaned towar
the captain. "Mr. Snyder is a detective, Captain Muller."

He looked up. It seemed to Mr. Snyder that a look of fear l
up his heavy eyes for an instant. It came and went, if indeed
came at all, so swiftly that he could not be certain.

"So?" said Captain Muller. He spoke quite evenly, with ju
the amount of interest which such an announcement woul
naturally produce.

"Now for yours, Captain," said Oakes. "I guess it's some
thing special. It's twice the size of mine, anyway."

It may have been something in the old woman's expressio
as she watched Captain Muller slowly tearing the paper tha

ent a thrill of excitement through Mr. Snyder. Something
eemed to warn him of the approach of a psychological mo-
ent. He bent forward eagerly.

There was a strangled gasp, a thump, and onto the table
rom the captain's hands there fell a little harmonica. There
vas no mistaking the look in Muller's face now. His cheeks
vere like wax, and his eyes, so dull till then, blazed with panic
nd horror which he could not repress. The glasses on the
able rocked as he clutched at the cloth.

Mrs. Pickett spoke. "Why, Captain Muller, has it upset you?
thought that, as his best friend, the man who shared his room,
ou would value a memento of Captain Gunner. How fond
ou must have been of him for the sight of his harmonica to be
uch a shock."

The captain did not speak. He was staring fascinated at the
hing on the table. Mrs. Pickett turned to Mr. Snyder. Her
yes, as they met his, held him entranced.

"Mr. Snyder, as a detective, you will be interested in a curi-
us and very tragic affair which happened in this house a few
ays ago. One of my boarders, Captain Gunner, was found
ead in his room. It was the room which he shared with Mr.
Muller. I am very proud of the reputation of my house, Mr.
nyder, and it was a blow to me that this should have hap-
ened. I applied to an agency for a detective, and they sent me
stupid boy, with nothing to recommend him except his belief
n himself. He said that Captain Gunner had died by accident,
illed by a snake which had come out of a crate of bananas. I
new better. I knew that Captain Gunner had been murdered.
Are you listening, Captain Muller? This will interest you, as
ou were such a friend of his."

The captain did not answer. He was staring straight before
im, as if he saw something invisible in eyes forever closed in
eath.

"Yesterday we found the body of a dog. It had been killed,
s Captain Gunner had been, by the poison of a snake. The
oy from the agency said that this was conclusive. He said that
e snake had escaped from the room after killing Captain
unner and had in turn killed the dog. I knew that to be im-

possible, for, if there had been a snake in that room it could not have made its escape."

Her eyes flashed and became remorselessly accusing. "It was not a snake that killed Captain Gunner. It was a cat. Captain Gunner had a friend who hated him. One day, in opening a crate of bananas, this friend found a snake. He killed it, and extracted the poison. He knew Captain Gunner's habits. He knew that he played a harmonica. This man also had a cat. He knew that cats hated the sound of a harmonica. He had often seen this particular cat fly at Captain Gunner and scratch him when he played. He took the cat and covered its claws with the poison. And then he left the cat in the room with Captain Gunner. He knew what would happen."

Oakes and Mr. Snyder were on their feet. Captain Muller had not moved. He sat there, his fingers gripping the cloth. Mrs. Pickett rose, and went to a closet. She unlocked the door. "Kitty!" she called. "Kitty! Kitty!"

A black cat ran swiftly out into the room. With a clatter and a crash of crockery and a ringing of glass the table heaved, rocked, and overturned as Muller staggered to his feet. He threw up his hands as if to ward something off. A choking cry came from his lips. "Gott! Gott!"

Mrs. Pickett's voice rang through the room, cold and biting. "Captain Muller, you murdered Captain Gunner!"

The captain shuddered. Then mechanically he replied. "Gott! Yes, I killed him."

"You heard, Mr. Snyder," said Mrs. Pickett. "He has confessed before witnesses."

Muller allowed himself to be moved toward the door. His arm in Mr. Snyder's grip felt limp. Mrs. Pickett stopped and took something from the debris on the floor. She rose, holding the harmonica.

"You are forgetting your souvenir, Captain Muller," she said.

MY FRIEND SAM

PENELOPE WALLACE

"I've read that there's a bond between a son and his
[m]other—but there certainly wasn't between Mum and me.

About the first thing I can remember is Mum telling a new
[fri]end about the awfulness of her pregnancy and the terrible
[ag]onies of labour and childbirth.

"And I said to Brian," she recounted, "I'm not going
[th]rough that again; not for anything. Of course he was disap-
[po]inted, but I'd given him a son"; she didn't add "such as he
[is]," but I know she felt it.

I don't remember what I wore in those days, but I do re-
[m]ember when I first went to school and my clothes were sev-
[er]al sizes too large.

"You'll grow into them," said Mum, and I did—and out of
[th]em.

Dad said I needed new shorts and Mum said we couldn't af-
[fo]rd it.

"He's going to be big like you," she told him. "Long arms
[an]d big feet. I can't keep up with him."

Dad was tall and I hoped I'd be just like him when I grew
[up]. He was gentle and kind, but I hoped I'd have a bit more
[fi]ght because he let Mum boss him; she was a slight five three
[bu]t she had a sharp tongue and a way of putting you in the
[w]rong.

My mate John, at school, says there's an old music hall
[so]ng about a little woman bossing a big man—his grandfather
[to]ld him about it. I hadn't got a grandfather but I had an
[au]nt—Dad's sister. Auntie Carrie was a lot like Dad and I was

very fond of her and not just because she gave me brilliant presents.

"Can't think where Carrie gets her money," said Mum. "She's unemployed but she spends money like water."

Dad said that Auntie Carrie liked spending her money, such as it was, on other people.

And that made me think. Mum spent money on herself, her clothes, "her" house—where it showed; but, basically, she was mean; and I understood why Grandad—Dad's father, who died when I was two—had taken out some sort of insurance to pay for my education; Mum would rather I went to a council school.

I think I was eight when I realised that. It was just before Sam came into my life. It was September and Sam was a black mongrel—still a puppy—with big brown eyes and a long feathery wagging tail. He followed me home one day on my way back from school.

Mum was out and he looked so hungry, so I wiped his paws with my handkerchief and took him into the kitchen. In the fridge there was some cold beef and I thought I could cut him a slice and Mum wouldn't notice. I found the carving knife and I didn't cut much. Sam wolfed the meat, then Mum came back and all hell broke loose. A dog in her kitchen and a mongrel at that; then she saw the joint and she was off again.

"He's my dog," I said without conviction.

As luck would have it, Dad came home early. He took it all in. Mum furious, Sam cowering in a corner, and me red with rage. I'd just told Mum that I hated her.

"Now Tom," he said, "I won't have talk like that. Apologise to your mother."

"I'm sorry, Mum," I said—but I wasn't.

Then I got the shock of my life because Dad took a tenner from his pocket and said to me:

"Go down to the shops and get some tins of dog food and collar and lead."

I ran all the way.

When I got back Dad was in the kitchen with Sam. We gave

him a bath in the sink and I put on his new collar; he looked beautiful.

Dad told me I'd have to get up early every morning and take Sam for a walk on the Common before I went to school, and a walk every night before I went to bed.

"I'll give you the money for his food," Dad told me, "and if you have to take him to the vet—like when he has his distemper jab—but anything else comes out of your pocket money. You put his meal up for him before you go to school and Mum'll put it down for him midday."

I didn't think Mum would like that but I didn't say anything.

"I rang the police station," he went on, "in case someone had reported him missing, but no one had."

He turned to Sam.

"By the look of you, no one's looked after you for quite a while."

Sam thumped his tail in agreement and Dad ran his hand over Sam's skinny ribs.

"I reckon someone turned him out," he said.

I don't know what Dad had said to Mum while I was off spending his tenner, but she only made one remark about Sam.

"He's going to be a big dog. He's got big feet."

Sam always kept as far away from Mum as he could; he knew she didn't like him.

I wondered whether Dad would go on standing up to Mum and I'd get some new trousers, but I didn't, so I guessed he'd made his once-in-a-lifetime gesture. Anyway, I'd rather have Sam and put up with the too-small clothes.

On Saturday afternoons and in the holidays, I'd take Sam on the Common for hours; sometimes Dad would come with us, and sometimes John would meet up with us and he and Sam and I would play on the Common.

Aunt Carrie came for Christmas; she said Sam was smashing and she went to the Common with Dad and me and Sam; we couldn't go very fast because she got puffed—Mum says it's because she's overweight and smokes—but we all had a great time.

After tea on Christmas Day, Mum said:

"We're going to Benidorm this summer. Don't know wha we'll do with the dog."

She never called him Sam.

"Kennels, I suppose," said Dad.

"Very expensive," snapped Mum, "we can't afford that."

She had a triumphant look and I thought she meant to tur Sam out. I put my arms round him. It was news to me abou Benidorm; we'd always gone to Eastbourne and I'd though Sam would come with us.

Auntie Carrie saved my life.

"No problem," she said, "I'll look after him."

"But Carrie," said Dad, "you've only got a small flat."

"Big enough for us two, and Sam's a well-behaved dog."

She turned to me.

"No Common in the city, but I'll walk him with his lea and I'll look after him."

I gave her a hug.

Dad looked happy and Mum looked furious.

Sam had grown a lot by the time he went to stay with Au Carrie; Mum was right—he was going to be a big dog.

Benidorm was boring and I missed Sam, but I enjoyed th flights even though we had to sit ages at the airport at bo ends.

Sam was happy to see me and we went up to the Commo to celebrate.

Time passed . . .

Sam grew to his full size. Auntie Carrie got more puffe but she still looked after him while we went to Benidorm Then, when I was thirteen, I met a German girl there—she w my age and Benidorm was not so boring; but I still misse Sam.

John and I stayed mates and sometimes on the Common w would meet other people exercising their dogs—especiall girls from the high school.

Now I am sixteen and Sam is eight, which is middle-age for a dog, and he doesn't run about as much, but he's still ve active. Next month we're off to Benidorm but Sam won't b going to stay with Aunt Carrie because, after Christmas, th overweight and the smoking took their toll and she died of a heart attack.

"What about the dog?" asked Mum.

"Kennels," replied Dad.

"And who's paying? You can't afford it and it's not as if your son's saved from a Saturday job *or* a holiday job."

"Rita, he was studying for his 'O' levels and he got eight— all *A*s and *B*s. Now he's working for his 'A' levels. He wouldn't have had time."

Good old Dad.

"What about the dog; it'll have to go."

"No," I said.

"It'll have to go sometime. You'll be going to college— waste of time but there we are—and if you think I'm going to look after it, you're very much mistaken."

"You mean have him put down?" asked Dad.

"No you can't . . ." I began.

"No," said Mum. "Vets cost money. It was lost before, it can be lost again."

"He wouldn't get lost round here," said Dad. "He'd just come home."

"Not here. I mean on the way to the airport."

Dad looked unhappy.

I felt physically sick.

I took Sam out for his evening walk. We walked a long way and I did a lot of thinking.

This morning we were all up early. As I put on Sam's collar, I could feel where Mum had prised off the nameplate.

Mum thinks of all the details.

I took Sam for a short walk, then we had breakfast and loaded the car. Mum got into the nearside rear seat of our four-door sedan and I got in beside her with Sam on his lead.

Dad is a good driver and we headed for Heathrow on the M.40, going fast in the middle lane with traffic behind us.

"I'm sorry, Sam," I told him, "I have to do this."

Mum opened the car door.

"Now," she said.

I heard the thump on the road, the squeal of brakes from the car following us, and the thump as it went over the body.

It was all over.

I wiped my forehead.

Maybe Dad will miss Mum, but not nearly as much as I'd have missed Sam.

THE CIRCUS MURDERS

EDWARD D. HOCH

The late summer of 1885 was a dangerous time for Ben
Snow. Even though Billy the Kid had been dead for four
years, the legend persisted that he had somehow survived the
shooting by Sheriff Pat Garrett at the old Maxwell ranch in the
New Mexico Territory. Ben's boyish face and lightning speed
with a gun had haunted him in those early days, and more than
once he'd been tagged as the dead Billy Bonney.

By September of '85, still only twenty-six years old, Ben
had ridden even farther to the Northeast, trying to put as much
space as possible between himself and New Mexico. Finally,
after boarding his new horse Oats at a stable west of Chicago,
he took the train east to Detroit and crossed over into Canada
at Windsor, Ontario. He figured on getting work there for the
winter, and then heading back West in the spring, when the interest in Billy the Kid might have died down.

But jobs weren't that easy to find for someone like Ben.
There was no need for a gunfighter or cowhand in Ontario.
"No cattle grazing around here," one employer told him, "ex-
cept for a few herd of dairy cows."

"There must be something I can do."

The man eyed him with a smirk. "How about a herd of elephants? Ever round up any of them?"

"Elephants?" Ben assumed the man was joking.

"The Barnum, Bailey & Hutchinson Circus is playing over
in Chatham, about forty miles east of here. They travel with
thirty-one elephants and always need extra handlers."

Ben was just young enough to be neither frightened nor of-

fended by the suggestion. He thanked the man politely and se
off for Chatham. His weapons and gunbelt were stowed safely
away in the bottom of his carpetbag and he might have been
any young man traveling in search of a job.

The train to Chatham deposited him not far from where the
circus was encamped for its brief stay. The railroad cars with
their Barnum, Bailey & Hutchinson signs were off on a siding
and the main tent was already in place. Ben strode through the
sawdust to the ticket booth where a young woman with dark
hair was preparing to open for business.

"Pardon me, Miss. Who would I see about a job?"

She eyed him up and down. "You an American? We'll be
going back across the border next week."

"I'm an American."

"All right—see my father, Colonel Jasper." She grinned a
little. "Tell him Anna sent you. His office is in that railroad
car."

"Thanks a lot."

Ben followed her direction and found himself in a plush
gaslit office, facing a stocky man with white muttonchop
whiskers who listened to him and then chuckled. "So my
daughter told you to see me. She mustn't think much of you
I've got no openings."

"Back in Windsor they told me you could always use an
elephant handler."

Colonel Jasper snorted. "A boy like you?"

"I'm twenty-six and I've done my share of range work. I've
handled steers that were probably as big as your elephants
sir."

The colonel stood up, laughing. "You think so? Follow me
son."

He led the way out the back to one of the railway cars fitted
out to carry animals. A few medium-sized elephants were
penned up out front, their ankles chained to heavy spikes
Colonel Jasper ignored them and led Ben around the back of
the car, where Ben came face to face with the largest creature
he'd ever seen.

It was an elephant, all right, but taller than anything he'd imagined. "It's twice as tall as I am!" he exclaimed.

"Almost. This is Jumbo, star of the show and the largest elephant in the world. We measure him at around eleven feet. Think you could handle him, son?"

"Maybe," Ben answered uncertainly.

Jasper laughed. "Don't worry, you won't have to. Jumbo has his own handler and keeper. Come here, Scotty."

A middle-aged man with dark eyes and a brown moustache hopped down from a bale of hay on which he'd been seated. For his age and weight, he moved with remarkable agility. "Yes sir, Colonel."

"Mr. Scott, this is Ben Snow. He wants a job handling the elephants. Think we can use him?"

The man the colonel called Scotty eyed Ben as the great elephant brushed the ground with its trunk in a kind of sweeping motion. "Have you had any experience with animals, Ben?"

"I've done ranch work out West with horses and cattle."

"A cowboy!"

"Sometimes," Ben admitted.

Colonel Jasper seemed satisfied. He quickly described Ben's wages and duties. "My daughter Anna handles the payroll. See her if you've got any questions."

Ben nodded. "Thank you, sir."

"Put him to work, Scotty."

When they were alone with the elephants, Scotty explained a bit about the job. "You don't have to worry about Jumbo here. I handle him personally. And Felix brings water for all the elephants. But the others need to be walked around, given a little exercise. Here, you can start with Tom Thumb. He's the smallest of them."

Ben was led over to meet Tom Thumb, a dwarf elephant who, Scotty explained, was something of a clown in the circus. "We usually bring him on with Jumbo, because there's such a difference between them."

As Ben played with the little elephant, he said, "Mr. Barnum's name's famous all over the country. Does he travel with you?"

Scotty shook his head. "Barnum spends most of his time

back in New York arranging bookings and handling business matters. Mr. Hutchinson is with us, but you're not likely to meet him. He leaves the ground work to his managers, like Colonel Jasper."

Scotty took Ben on a tour of the main tent, where customers were beginning to fill the seats for the afternoon performance. "It's a big place," Ben said. He'd never seen an enclosed space quite as large before.

"Holds twenty thousand people and we fill it twice a day, for the afternoon and evening performances. Three of the four rings are in constant use, with different acts being performed simultaneously."

Ben was suddenly aware that Scotty didn't talk like the other Americans he knew. His experience with accents was limited but he took a good guess. "Are you English, Scotty?"

"Sure am. I was Jumbo's favorite keeper at the London Zo-ological Gardens—which is where he came from. He came from Africa originally, by way of Paris, but he was in London for seventeen years."

"How did Barnum get him over here?"'

"That's a long story I'll tell you someday. Meanwhile, watch your step, Ben."

"You mean with Colonel Jasper?"

"I don't know exactly what I mean. He wouldn't tell you this, but the man you're replacing was murdered two days ago. Nobody knows who did it."

After that, Ben wasn't satisfied until he had the entire story, which Scotty told him with some reluctance.

The man's name had been Rusty Gallagher and, like Ben, he'd been something of a drifter. He'd been on the job since June, traveling across the northern states with the circus, tend-ing to the elephants with Scotty and Felix. Two nights before, in Windsor, he'd been found dead next to Jumbo's enclosure, his skull crushed as if by a blow or a fall. Mr. Hutchinson and Colonel Jasper had hushed the matter up, using a few well placed bribes to convince local police that the death was acci-dental. Otherwise, as Scotty explained it, the entire circus could have been stuck in Windsor awaiting the outcome of an inquest. Jumbo was too big an attraction to have this death hanging over him.

"You mean they think Jumbo killed him?" Ben said.

"Some folks do," Scotty admitted. "But not me. He's the gentlest animal I've ever known—perfect around children. They climb all over his back and it never bothers him."

"Maybe this Gallagher fellow was tormenting him."

"No. Whoever killed him, it wasn't Jumbo," Scotty said.

It was one of Scotty's duties to parade Tom Thumb and Jumbo into the main tent for their initial appearance together, and as the afternoon performance got under way he went off to prepare the elephants.

The elephants' water boy, Felix Knight, was hardly a boy— he must have been close to fifty. He walked with a limp, which he told Ben he'd gotten fighting for the North at the Second Battle of Bull Run. "We lost that time, too," he said with resignation. "I was out of the war for good before the tide turned and the Union started winning."

"Do you carry water for all these elephants?" Ben asked.

"Yes. It's not so bad this time of year. In the summer when it's hot and they're thirsty, I get some of the town kids to help out. Pay 'em with passes to the circus."

"Are the bosses here good to work for?"

Felix shrugged, emptying his pails of water into Jumbo's trough as he spoke. "They're as good as any. The best of the lot is the colonel's daughter. She makes a man feel young again."

She did indeed, and when she stopped Ben for payroll information later that afternoon he felt that he'd known her for years. She brushed the dark hair back from her eyes and said, "You can go watch the performance, you know. It'll give you an idea of what everyone does here."

She must have been about Ben's own age, perhaps a few years younger, but traveling with the circus had given her a worldliness that surprised him. Until then his experience with women had been limited to ranchers' daughters and the prostitutes you encountered in any frontier town. "I might do that, Miss Jasper," he said.

"I'm just Anna around here," she told him.

"It must be exciting, traveling around like you do, seeing a different town every few days."

"You get tired of it," she said. "The animals keep me interested, though. I love the animals."

"Is it true that Jumbo killed a man the other day?"

Her eyes flashed. "No, that's not true! Jumbo is the kindest, gentlest elephant I've ever known. The children love him, just as they loved him back at the London zoo."

"If they loved him so much, why was he sold to Barnum?"

"That needn't concern you," Anna told him.

Ben decided to change the subject. "Was your father a colonel in the war?"

"He was on President Lincoln's personal staff in Washington," she told him with a touch of pride, recovering her good spirits. "I was only a baby at the time, of course, but my mother used to tell me about it."

"Does she travel with the show, too?"

"No, she's back home in Pennsylvania."

They'd strolled over to a flap in the main tent, which suddenly parted to reveal two identical young men in spangled tights running out to the sound of applause. Anna grabbed them both by the arm. "Wait a minute, I want you to meet Ben Snow. He's going to be helping Scotty and Felix with the elephants. Ben, these are the Twinkle Twins—Tommy and Terry—the best tumblers in the business."

"Glad to meet you," Tommy said with a strong southern accent. "How you gettin' on with Jumbo?"

"Fine so far," Ben told him. He watched them head for one of the railway cars. "Are their names *really* Twinkle?"

Anna laughed. "No, of course not. My father discovered them down in Alabama last year. Wait till you see them perform."

Through the flap, Ben saw a parade of clowns and jugglers, acrobats and bareback riders. "Where do you find all these people?" he marveled.

"Some of the best performers are European. Our star bareback rider is Bavarian, and we have a Tattooed Man from Greece."

Scotty appeared behind them and tapped Ben on the shoulder. "Let's go, Ben. The elephants are on next."

Ben soon discovered that although the handlers carried long whips it was rarely necessary to use them in putting the elephants through their paces. "They're mostly for loading them onto the train," Scotty explained, showing him how to handle the whip. "These elephants are born performers, so long as you give them plenty of food and water and don't do anything to torment them."

"Do you think that's what happened to Rusty Gallagher? Was he tormenting Jumbo?"

"I told you no. And Jumbo didn't kill him."

"Who were Rusty's friends here?" Ben persisted.

"I don't know. He made overtures to Anna, but just about everyone does that until they discover she's unavailable." Ben wondered if that was for his benefit. "I suppose he was friendly with the Twinkle Twins. They came from the same hometown."

That night, at the show's evening performance, Scotty and Ben led Jumbo and some of the other elephants in the grand entry and promenade, during which most of the troupe marched three times around the main tent, between the banked-earth rings and the spectators' seats, while the band played a rousing introduction. Mr. Hutchinson led the promenade, mounted astride a prancing white horse, and Ben doubted that even Barnum himself could have been a more imposing figure.

Later, as he helped Scotty wash down Jumbo, Ben reminded him, "You were going to tell me how Jumbo got here from the London zoo. Anna bristled a little when I asked her why the zoo sold him to Barnum."

"It's a sad story in a way." Scotty scrubbed the elephant's back with a long-handled brush. "Everyone in London loved Jumbo. He was the largest elephant in the world and still is, far as I know, but he was so gentle with children they could feed him a biscuit or a lump of sugar and he took it with the delicacy of an English matron at teatime. But at the London zoo he displayed an uncertain temper when he was by himself in the elephant house. Some of the directors were afraid there might be a latent streak of insanity that might one day surface—they were uneasy about trusting small children within reach of his ponderous trunk, even though he was always gentle around them. When the offer came from Barnum, they decided to accept it and avoid the possibility of a future tragedy."

"How much did Barnum pay?" Ben asked.

"Two thousand pounds. That's around ten thousand dollars. It cost Barnum twice that to have him shipped to America. The iron-bound box took up two decks of the *Assyrian Monarch,* and since the ship was forbidden to carry passengers on those decks Barnum had to reimburse the company for its lost business on the voyage. But the worst part came when I started to lead Jumbo from the zoo down to the ship. As soon as he felt the unfamiliar ground underfoot, he refused to go any farther. We'd already had a bad scene the previous day when they tried to chain him. The press made so much of it it intensified the indignation of the public, who were already displeased about the sale to Barnum. Queen Victoria intervened and urged that Jumbo be kept at the zoo regardless of the contract. It took a five-week lawsuit to settle the affair. Barnum finally won the elephant and hired me to come with him to America. I succeeded in luring Jumbo on board the ship with his favorite buns and a little beer."

"Beer!"

Scotty chuckled at Ben's reaction. "His daily ration in London was two hundred pounds of hay, five pails of water, and a quart of whiskey. I thought I did very well cutting him back to beer. It was a rough two-week crossing that April, but he came through it fine. He was taken immediately to Madison Square Garden in New York, where the circus was playing. The crowds he attracted more than paid for the cost of the journey."

"He's never been back to London since?"

"No. Barnum promised to take him back someday, but I believe that was only to mollify the British public."

"He's shown no sign of his bad temper since being with the circus?"

Scotty looked at Ben coolly. "Nothing that would endanger a human being, if that's what you mean."

That night after the line of horses with their plumes and spangles and tasseled blankets had made one last circle of the four rings, it was time to pack up for the next stop on the tour.

"St. Thomas," Anna told Ben when he asked. "It's about sixty miles farther along, on the way to a stop in London, Ontario."

Striking the tents, securing the animals, and loading the equipment into the freight cars took more time than Ben had expected. Working in near darkness was new and difficult for him, and even though the loading of the animals had begun while the performance was still under way, there was still much to be done. Jumbo and Tom Thumb took part in the finale, so they were the last of the elephants to be loaded on board. Scotty had Jumbo under control and Ben was urging Tom Thumb forward when the midget elephant ran into one of the burly roustabouts, knocking him to the ground. The sight of it was so funny that Ben made matters worse by laughing.

The roustabout was on his feet, fists clenched. "What's so funny, cowboy?"

"I just—"

The worker swung at Ben, catching him with a right to the jaw. He went backward into the sawdust, but was on his feet at once, keeping his head low as he charged the roustabout.

"Stop that, you two!" Scotty came running as Ben butted the man and went down on top of him. Ben was pulling back his fist when Scotty grabbed both his arms and yanked him off the other man.

"That's Kirt Flagon," Scotty warned under his breath. "He'd as soon kill you as look at you."

"I owe him one," Ben protested, trying to shake off Scotty's restraining hands.

"Yeah, and if you pay it off he'll be waiting for you behind the train some night with a sharpened tent peg."

Flagon gave Ben a long, mean look and then allowed himself to be led away by his friends.

*   *   *

"Most circuses still travel by wagon," Scotty explained as their train pulled into the St. Thomas yards before dawn. "But Barnum says trains are the way to go. We can move by night and everyone gets at least a few hours' sleep. And we can cover distances faster, too. With wagons we'd never be able to play as many small one-night performances as we do. There's always something breaking down. Not to mention the problem of getting thirty-one elephants into wagons. Most of them would end up walking, and that would add to the delay."

"Circuses are pretty rare where I come from," Ben admitted. "We get some medicine shows and an occasional trained-bear act, but that's about all."

Scotty climbed out of the bunk and Ben heard his bare feet hit the floor. "Let's get going. We can move the elephants out before daybreak."

Once the ramp was in place for them, Ben found that the elephants were only too anxious to leave the boxcars for firm ground. He was leading the first batch to their new enclosures when one of the Twinkle Twins hurried by. "Have you seen my brother?" he asked Ben.

"No. Which one are you?"

"Tommy—I'm looking for Terry." He hurried on, looking anxious.

The sky was beginning to glow on the eastern horizon, and already small boys from the town were running up to watch the circus unloading. They gave a cheer when Scotty led Jumbo off his special car and he had to warn them to keep out of the way. The great elephant flapped its ears and trumpeted a greeting, which brought another cheer.

"Look alive here," Colonel Jasper shouted to no one in particular, hurrying along the track. "We've got work to do!"

"Colonel," Scotty called to him, "what's that other track for? You know it's dangerous to lead the animals across track."

"They tell me it's an unused spur line. There won't be any trains along it."

Scotty seemed satisfied and continued with the unloading. Ben was especially careful with Tom Thumb, remembering the previous night's trouble. But there was no sign of Kirt

Flagon near the train and Ben only spotted him later driving pegs for the main tent. By that time he'd encountered Tommy Twinkle again. "Did you find your brother?" he asked him.

"Yes." Tommy gave Ben a toothy grin. "He was with one of the girls."

When all the elephants were in their enclosures, Ben helped Felix unload hay that had been purchased in town to feed the animals. "They'll be thirsty after this load," Ben said, heaving a bale into Jumbo's pen.

"Lake Erie's just a few miles away if we need it," Felix replied with a laugh.

Later, as the afternoon performance got under way, Ben helped Scotty and Felix with the elephants. After his initial appearance, which never failed to evoke cheers and applause, Jumbo was brought back to his pen for feeding and watering. Felix went off to fetch the water buckets while Scotty supervised Ben in getting some of the other elephants ready. The lions and tigers seemed unusually restless in their nearby cages and Ben cast a wary eye in their direction. "Are they always this noisy?"

Scotty shrugged. "Every town is different. The odors are different. It takes them a while to settle down."

One of the clowns ran up to tell Scotty the tumblers weren't in their ring. Scotty cursed. "Stay here and look after Jumbo, Ben, while I hunt up Colonel Jasper. We may have to bring the elephants on earlier than usual."

As soon as Scotty had disappeared from sight, Ben heard Jumbo making a terrible commotion on the other side of the enclosure. Deciding that the other elephants could be left for a moment in their ankle chains, he ran around to see what the trouble was.

Lying inside Jumbo's pen, virtually under the feet of the great elephant, was the bloodied body, in his spangled costume, of one of the Twinkle Twins.

Word of the death spread like wildfire among the circus people, though they did their best to keep the news from reaching the spectators at the afternoon performance. No mention was made of the Twinkle Twins, and even Jumbo's absence from the finale went virtually unnoticed. When one family asked Colonel Jasper about it on the way out, he merely replied that their big attraction was a bit under the weather.

The local police had been summoned, of course, and they'd ordered that Jumbo remain chained until their investigation was complete. As he'd done following the previous death, Scotty argued vigorously in the elephant's defense and Colonel Jasper joined in. At one point Mr. Hutchinson appeared, looking distraught. "What's going on here, Colonel? Two killings within a week and no explanation? Who was killed this time?"

"One of the twin tumblers. We're not sure which one because we haven't been able to locate the other twin."

Hutchinson was obviously frustrated. "I don't want to telegraph Mr. Barnum about this if I don't have to."

"Where is he?" Jasper asked.

"At the Murray Hill Hotel in New York City."

"Let's wait until we know the facts," the colonel suggested. Ben was standing on one side with Felix Knight and he called them both over. "What do you know about it?" he asked them.

"I was out getting water for Jumbo," Felix told him. "I'd just filled the buckets when I heard the commotion. I dropped them and came running when Ben called for help."

Colonel Jasper shook his head sadly. "Is there any possible chance Jumbo could have done it?"

"No, sir!" Scotty insisted. "I'd stake my life on it. He never harmed a living being, and he hasn't changed now!"

"There was some concern at your zoo in London at the time he was sold. He was said to have a bad temper."

"Only in the elephant house. Perhaps he didn't like it there for one reason or another. He's been with the circus here for nearly three and a half years without anything like this happening."

Colonel Jasper turned back to Ben. "Couldn't you see anything from where you stood?"

"No, sir. I was at the other end of the elephant enclosure. You know we hang sheets of canvas between the pens to help keep the animals calm."

"What about this missing twin? Have you any idea where e could be?"

Ben shook his head. "But they were ready to go on, sir, in heir spangled tights. The missing twin couldn't have gone far n that costume."

"Perhaps not," said Hutchinson. "Colonel, I want you to or-;anize search parties at once. We have three hours until the vening performance and we've got to use every minute of it."

Ben found an empty bucket and brought Jumbo some water, ut the big elephant wasn't thirsty. Instead, he stood curling nd uncurling his trunk, occasionally trumpeting his displea-ure at all the activity around him. Watching the searchers set-ing off to find the missing twin, Ben had his own idea of vhere the man might be.

Anna Jasper was at the box-office counter totaling the after-oon's receipts. "Did you hear what happened?" he asked.

"Isn't it terrible? Do they know which twin it is yet?"

"They don't, but I think I might."

She looked blank. "How?"

"I saw Tommy earlier," he explained. "He said he was look-ng for Terry. Then later he told me he'd found Terry with a irl. I think Tommy might be dead and Terry might be hiding vith the girl."

Anna was dubious. "That's not much to go on."

"What girl has Terry been seeing, do you know?"

She hesitated and then said, "Sandra. She's one of the rapeze artists."

"Where does she sleep?"

"On the train. I can show you." She scooped up the money nd stuffed it into a leather pouch. "Come on."

Sandra was a pretty redhead who was changing into her treet clothes when Anna knocked at the wall by her berth and nnounced herself. Ben hovered behind, waiting to see how he conversation would go. "We're looking for Terry," Anna old her. "His brother's been killed."

"I heard. What makes you think Terry would be here?"

"Just a hunch," Ben said, moving in. He pushed Anna gen-

tly aside and lunged for the upper berth, where he'd see
something move among the blankets. It was one of the twin
in his spangled costume.

"No!" he shouted. "Leave me alone! I don't want to die!"

Ben had to drag him out of the berth down onto the floo
"You're not going to die."

"He'll kill me next, I know he will!"

"Who? Jumbo?"

"Jumbo didn't kill anybody."

"Then tell us who did."

He was trembling with fright. "No, no, I can't!"

"Come along, then. They need you to identify your brothe
I won't let anyone hurt you."

The redhead told Anna, "He's been like this since he cam
here an hour ago. He said Tommy'd just been killed and he'
be next. He insisted I hide him."

But Terry would say nothing more. He allowed himself t
be returned to the elephant area outside the main tent and h
identified the body of his brother in a soft, almost inaudibl
voice, then he left again with Sandra. He seemed to trust n
one else near him, including Anna.

The local authorities were unwilling to accept Terry's wor
that his brother had been murdered. But Ben spotted some
thing the others had missed. There was a tent peg half burie
in the sawdust, and when he picked it up he saw bloodstair
on the broad end. "Does this satisfy you?" he asked, holding
up. "Or do you think Jumbo swung this with his trunk?"

The local sheriff impounded it as evidence, and it strengtl
ened Terry's words. "I'm convinced," Mr. Hutchinson ar
nounced. "Jumbo will perform tonight. I don't believe he'
harmed anyone."

Scotty grinned and patted the elephant's trunk.

During the break between shows, Anna Jasper allowed Be
to escort her into the town of St. Thomas for something to ea
"Usually I don't mind eating with the others," she told hin
"but tonight I just wanted to get away. There's somethin
going on that frightens me."

"I think it's frightening everyone," Ben said. "Especiall

Terry. Did you notice how he even seemed afraid of you after we found him?"

"I think you're right," she agreed, avoiding his eyes.

"How could that be, when he indicated the killer was a man?"

She was silent for a time, picking at her food. Finally she forced herself to answer. "He thinks my father might be involved."

"The colonel? That's crazy."

She said no more at first, and then she added only, "Ben, you and I are too young to remember the war, and the depth of the hatred it caused on both sides . . ."

There was no way of knowing what rumors had spread among the townsfolk about the latest killing and Jumbo's possible involvement, but there was a sellout crowd for that evening's performance. Ben was in charge of Tom Thumb during the early part of the show and watched with pleasure as the dwarf elephant cavorted with the clowns.

The circus was due in London, Ontario, the following day, so it was important that Ben begin loading some of the elephants before the performance ended. Scotty had said he'd bring Jumbo and Tom Thumb after the finale and Ben was waiting for them when he encountered the roustabout, Kirt Flagon.

"Well, if it isn't the cowboy again," Flagon said, feigning surprise. He carried a tent peg in one hand, the narrow end sharpened to a daggerlike point.

"Haven't we had enough violence here for one day?" Ben asked, wishing he'd unpacked his six-shooter.

"This'll be the last of it," Flagon assured him, lunging forward.

Ben sidestepped and hit the man on the back of the neck as he went by. Flagon tottered but didn't fall. In an instant they were locked together, grappling for the sharpened tent peg.

Suddenly the shrill blast of a train whistle cut through the night. Ben looked up to see a locomotive and several cars rounding a bend on the track that was said to be unused. He broke free of Flagon's grasp and shouted a warning at the figures on the track. Then the light of the locomotive straightened

and targeted them with its beam, and Ben saw to his horror
that Scotty had Jumbo and Tom Thumb headed back to their
cars, directly in the path of the oncoming train.

Hemmed in by the circus train on one side and a steep ditch
on the other, Scotty had nowhere to go but forward. He urged
the two elephants on, trying to outrun the train as the warning
whistle sounded again. Ben could see that the engineer had applied the brakes, but the locomotive was on a downgrade and
the distance was too short. The train hit Tom Thumb a glancing blow, knocking the dwarf elephant into the ditch, and then
plowed into Jumbo's hind legs.

The huge elephant gave a terrible roar that Ben would remember for the rest of his life, then went down as the locomotive jumped the track and passed over him.

It took Jumbo fifteen minutes to die, while crews labored to
remove him from under the train. He groaned only once before
life left him, and even then Scotty stayed with him, sobbing
against the body of the great elephant.

While veterinary surgeons labored over Tom Thumb, the
others headed back to the tent. The accident had occurred
around nine-thirty and by ten o'clock an informal group had
gathered by Jumbo's empty pen to listen to Mr. Hutchinson.
"This is a great tragedy for us all," he said. "I've already
telegraphed Mr. Barnum in New York. We'll spend the night
here and leave for London in the morning. There are audiences
waiting there and the show will have to go on without Jumbo."

"What about the killings?" Anna asked.

Mr. Hutchinson looked somber. "If Jumbo was responsible—"

"No," Ben said, stepping forward. "We owe that noble beast
this much, at least—to clear his name of any hint of scandal.
Jumbo never killed anyone. I showed you that bloody tent peg
this afternoon."

"He's right," Terry Twinkle said. Ben hadn't noticed him
standing to one side in his regular clothes. "My brother was
killed for the same reason Rusty Gallagher was—because
we're different from the rest of you. We talk different. We're
from the South. And Colonel Jasper hated us for that."

The colonel took a step forward but his daughter held him back. "My father never harmed anyone!" she shouted at Terry. "Not even in the war!"

"Then why else were they killed?"

It was time for Ben to speak again. "Quiet down, everyone. I've only been with you for two days, but there are a few things about these killings that are clear to me. First, Jumbo is innocent. Second, and here I agree with Terry, the only thing the victims seem to have had in common was that they were both from the same Alabama town. They could have been killed because they were southerners. But if that's the case, there's a far more likely suspect among you than Colonel Jasper, who fought the entire war behind a desk in Washington. There's one man here who was wounded at Bull Run, who never took part in the North's great victories, who may have nurtured a hatred of the South that he was finally unable to suppress."

It was Colonel Jasper who gave a name to the accusation. "You're talking about Felix Knight."

"Exactly."

Felix had been lingering near the edge of the group. "What are you talking about?" he said.

"At first I had my suspicions of Kirt Flagon, the roustabout," Ben said. "He's a violent man who picks fights easily, and a tent peg seems to be his favorite weapon. But I learned a little while ago that he prefers the narrow end, sharpened to a point, rather than the blunt end. And then I remembered something about Felix. He'd gone to get water for Jumbo shortly before Tommy's murder. He would have arrived back with the pails just about the time the killing took place."

"Except that I didn't," Felix insisted. "I told you I was still filling the buckets when I heard the commotion."

Ben nodded. "I know what you said, but it wasn't true. After we found the body. I fetched a pail of water for Jumbo myself, but he wasn't thirsty. How could that be, I wondered, when he consumed five buckets a day and hadn't had any since the bale of hay that would certainly have made him thirsty? Since you were the only one who brought water to

Jumbo, there was just one possible explanation. You lied. You did give Jumbo water. And that places you at the scene of the murder just when it happened. You had no reason to lie about it unless you killed Tommy."

This time Felix had a knife, but he didn't leap at Ben. He went instead for Terry. "Now I'll finish the job!" he cried, and he almost did before they managed to drag him off.

It was Mr. Hutchinson who brought them the only good news of the night. The veterinary surgeons reported that Tom Thumb's left hind leg was broken but otherwise he was all right. The leg was being set and he would be able to make the trip to London, Ontario, with the others. Even Scotty managed a weak smile at the news.

Ben knew he wouldn't remain long with the circus. He needed the open spaces and freedom of the West. He hoped for one more chance at Kirt Flagon before he departed, but that was not to be. The roustabout was jailed by the local police in London after starting a barroom brawl and Ben never saw him again.

DOGS

LOREN D. ESTLEMAN

Elda Chase lived in an efficiency flat in Iroquois Heights with no rugs on the hardwood floor and the handsome furniture arranged in geometric patterns like a manor house maze. That day she had the curtains open on the window overlooking the municipal park and the statue of LaSalle with his foot up on a rock scratching his head over a map he had unrolled on his knee. The view was strictly for my benefit; Elda Chase had been blind since birth.

Not that you'd have known it from the way she got around that apartment, discreetly touching this chair and brushing that lamp as she bustled to catch the whistling teapot and find the cups and place the works on a platter and bring it over and set it down on the coffee table. When I leaned forward from the sofa to pour, I was just in time to accept the full cup she extended to me. She filled the other one then and took a seat in the chair opposite. She was a tall woman in her middle fifties who wore her graying hair pinned up and lightly tinted glasses with clear plastic rims. Her ruby blouse and long matching skirt went well with her high coloring and she had on pearl earrings and white low-heeled shoes. I wondered who picked it all out.

"The Braille edition of the Yellow Pages comes so late," she said, balancing her cup and saucer on one crossed knee. "I was half afraid your number had changed."

"Not in a dozen years. Or anything else about the office, except the wallpaper."

"Anyway, thank you for coming. You were the fourth in-

vestigator I tried. The first number was disconnected and th
other two men referred me to the Humane Society. I'd calle
them right after it happened, of course. They wanted me to pu
up posters around the neighborhood. As if I could go out at al
without my Max."

"Max is the dog?"

"A shepherd. I've had him three years. When Lucy died
was sure I'd never have another one as good, but Max is spe
cial. He's taken me places I'd never have dared go witl
Lucy."

I sipped some tea and was relieved to find out it was bitter
Watching her operate I'd begun to feel inadequate. "You're
sure he didn't run away?"

"Trained seeing-eye dogs don't run away, Mr. Walker. Bu
to lay your cynicism to rest, the padlock on the kennel doo
had been cut. You saw it in the yard?"

"A six-foot chain link fence to keep in a dog that wouldn'
run away," I confirmed.

"The fence was to protect him. It didn't do a very good job
I knew dog-stealing was a possibility, but I hate to keep a biş
animal cooped up indoors. The police were not encouraging."

"I'm not surprised, in this town."

"I like Iroquois Heights," she said.

"The park is nice."

She raised her face. With her sightless eyes downcast be
hind the colored lenses she looked like a lioness taking in th
sun. "Can you find him?"

"There are markets for purebreds. I can ask some questions
I can't promise anything. My specialty's tracing two-legge
mammals."

"I could have gone to someone who traces pets for a living
I don't like professional dog people. They're strident. They'
make me out the villain for not hiring a governess to look afte
the dog."

"Is there a picture?"

She groped for and opened a drawer in the end table next to
her chair and handed me a color snapshot of herself in a wrap
and gloves hanging on to a harness attached to a black and ta
German shepherd.

"Marks?" I put it in my breast pocket.

"Now, how would I know that?"

"Sorry. I forgot."

"I'll take that as a compliment. He answers to his name with a sharp bark." She took a checkbook off the end table and started writing. "Seven-fifty is your retainer, I believe."

I took the check and put it in my wallet. I drank some more tea, peeled my upper lip back down, and stood, setting aside the cup and saucer. "I'll call you tomorrow. Earlier if I find out anything."

"Thank you." She hesitated. "It isn't just that I need him. If it were just that—"

"I had a dog once," I said. "I still think about him sometimes."

"You sound like someone who would."

Mrs. Chase's landlady, a thin blonde named Silcox, lived on the ground floor. Mrs. Chase was her oldest tenant and Mrs. Silcox's son, a sophomore at the University of Michigan, had built the kennel at his mother's request. Neither was home when it was broken into.

From there I went to the office of the Iroquois Heights *Spectator*. The newspaper was the flagship of a fleet owned by a local politician, but the classified section was reliable. I asked for that editor and was directed to a paunchy grayhead standing at the water cooler.

"Rube Zendt," he said when I introduced myself, and shook my hand. "Born Reuben, but trust newspaper folk to latch on to the obvious."

His hair was thin and black on top with gray sidewalls and he had a chipmunk grin that was too small for his full cheeks. He wore black-rimmed glasses and a blue tie at half-mast on a white shirt. I apologized for interrupting his break.

"This distilled stuff rusts my pipes. I only come here to watch the bubbles. Got something to sell or buy, or did you lose something or find it?"

"Close. A local woman hired me to find her dog. I thought that holding down lost and found you'd be the one to talk to about the local market."

"Dog-napping, you mean. I just take the ads. Man you want to see is Stillwell on cophouse."

"He around?"

"This time of day you can catch him at the police station."

"What time of day can I catch him anywhere else?"

The chipmunk grin widened a hundredth of an inch. "I see you know our town. But things aren't so bad down there since Mark Proust made acting chief."

"Meaning what?"

"Meaning he spends all his time in his office. Tell Stillwell Rube sent you."

The first three floors of a corner building on the main stem belonged to the city police. It was a hot day in August and the air conditioning was operating on the ground floor, but that had nothing to do with the drop in my temperature when I came in from the street. At the peak of the busing controversy in the early seventies a group of local citizens had protested the measure by overturning a bus full of schoolchildren; some of that group were in office now and they had built the city law-enforcement structure from the prosecutor right down to the last meter maid.

A steely-haired desk sergeant with an exotropic eye turned the good one on me from behind his high bench when I said I was looking for Stillwell of the *Spectator* and held it on me for another minute before saying, "Over there."

The wandering eye was pointing north and I went that way. He'd never have made the Detroit department with that eye, but with his temperament he was right at home.

Two big patrolmen in light summer uniforms were fondling their saps in the corner by the men's room, leering at and listening to a man with no hair above the spread collar of his shirt and a wrinkled cotton sport coat over it.

". . . and the other guy says 'Help me find my keys and we'll *drive* out of here!' "

The cops opened a pair of mouths like buckets and roared. I approached the bald man. "Mr. Stillwell?"

The laughter stopped like a bell grabbed in mid-clang. Two

pairs of cop eyes measured me and the bald man's face went guarded with the jokester's leer still in place. "Who's asking?"

"Amos Walker. Rube Zendt said to talk to you."

"Step into my office." He pushed open the men's room door and held it. The cops moved off.

The place had two urinals, a stall, and a sink. He leaned his shoulders against the stall, waiting. He was younger than the clean head indicated, around thirty. He had no eyebrows and clear blue eyes in a lineless face whose innocence could turn the oldest filthy joke into a laugh marathon. I gave him my spiel.

"Shepherd," he said. "There's not a lot of call for them without papers. No gold rushes going on in Alaska to goose the sled-dog trade."

"It's a seeing eye. That's an expensive market."

"They're handled by big organizations that train their own. They don't need to deal in stolen animals and you'd need papers and a good story to sell them one that's already schooled. Tell your client to place an ad with Rube offering a reward and stay home and wait to hear from whoever took the dog."

"Staying home is no problem."

"I guess not. Sorry I can't help."

"What about the fight game?"

"There's no fight game in this town."

"What town we talking about."

"Yeah." He crossed his ankles then and I knew my leg had been pulled. "That racket's all pit bulls now. I can think of only one guy would even look at a shepherd."

I gave him twenty dollars.

"Henry Revere." He crumpled the bill into the side pocket of his sport coat. "Caretaker over at the old high school. He's there days."

"School board know what he does nights?"

"Everyone knows everything that goes on in this town, except the people who pay taxes to live in it."

"Thanks." I gave him a card, which he crumpled into the same pocket without looking at it. Coming out of the men's room I had the desk sergeant's errant eye. The other was on a woman in a yellow pants suit who had come in to complain about a delivery van that was blocking her Coup de Ville in her driveway.

It was a three story brick box with big mullioned windows and a steel tube that slanted down from the roof for a fire escape. When the new school was built down the road, this one had been converted into administrative offices and a place to vote in district elections. I found its only inhabitant on that summer vacation day, an old black man wearing a green worksuit and tennis shoes, waxing the gym floor. He saw me coming in from the hall and turned off the machine. "Street shoes!"

I stopped. He left the machine and limped my way. I saw that the sole of one of his sneakers was built up twice as thick as its mate.

"Mister, you know how hard it is to get black heel marks off of hardwood?"

"Sorry." I showed him my I.D. "I'm looking for a German shepherd, answers to Max. If you're Henry Revere, someone told me you deal in them."

"Someone lied. What use I got for dogs? I got a job."

"Also a lot of girlfriends. Unless those are dog hairs on your pants."

He caught himself looking, too late. His cracked face bunched like a fist. "You're trespassing."

I held up two ten-dollar bills. He didn't look at them.

"This here's a good job, mister. I got a wife with a bad cough and a boy at Wayne State. I ain't trading them for no twenty bucks. You better get out before I call the po-lice"

I put away the bills. "What are you afraid of?"

"Unemployment and welfare," he said. "Maybe you never been there."

Back in my office in downtown Detroit I made some calls. First I rang Elda Chase, who said that no one had called her yet offering to return Max for a reward. I tried the Humane Society in three counties and got a female shepherd, a mix, and a lecture about the importance of spaying and neutering one's pets at sixty bucks a crack. After that it was time for dinner. When I got back from the place down the street the telephone was ringing. I said hello twice.

"Walker?"

"This is Walker."

Another long pause. "Ed Stillwell. The *Spectator?*"

I said I remembered him. He sounded drunk.

"Yeah. Listen, what I told you 'bout Henry Revere? Forget it. Bum steer."

"I don't think so. He denied too much when I spoke to him."

There was a muffled silence on his end, as of a hand clamped over the mouthpiece. Then: "Listen. Forget it, okay? I only gave you his name 'cause I needed the twenty. I got to make a monthly spousal support payment you wouldn't believe. What I know about dogfighting you could stick in a whistle."

"Okay."

" 'Kay."

A receiver was fumbled into the cradle. I hung up and sat there smoking a couple of cigarettes before I went home.

". . . believe the motive was robbery. Once again, Iroquois Heights journalist Edward Stillwell, in critical condition this morning at Detroit General Hospital after police found him beaten unconscious in an empty lot next to the *Spectator* building."

I had turned on the radio while fixing breakfast and got the end of the story. I tried all the other stations. Nothing. I turned off the stove and called the *Spectator*. I kept getting a busy signal. I settled for coffee and left home. As I swung out of the driveway, a navy blue Chrysler with twin mounted spotlights and no chrome pulled away from the curb behind me.

It was still in my mirror when I found a slot in front of the *Spectator* office. I went inside, where everyone on the floor was hunched over his desk arguing with a telephone. Rube Zendt hung his up just as I took a seat in the chair in front of his desk. "The damn *Free Press*," he said, pointing at the instrument. "They want the rundown on Stillwell before we even print it. Those city sheets think they wrote the First Amendment."

"Which desk is Stillwell's?"

"Why?"

I counted on my fingers. "Stillwell gives me a man to see about a dog. A cross-eyed sergeant at the cophouse sees us talking. I see the man. Last night Stillwell calls me, sounding sloshed and telling me to forget the man. This morning the cops scrape Stillwell out of an alley."

"Empty lot."

"In Detroit we call them alleys. I'm not finished. This morning I've got a tail that might as well have UNMARKED PO-LICE CAR painted in big white letters on the side. Someone's scared. I want to know what makes Stillwell so scary. Maybe he kept notes. He's a newspaperman."

"I can't let you go through his desk. Only Stillwell can do that. Or George Strong. He publishes the *Spectator*."

"I know who Strong is. Where is he?"

"Lady, we don't *need* no warrant. We're in hot pursuit of a suspect in an assault and battery."

This was a new player. I turned in my chair and looked at a pair of hulks in strained jackets and wide ties standing just inside the front door dwarfing a skinny woman in a tailored suit. One, a crewcut blond with a neck like a leg, spotted me and pointed. "There he is."

I got up. "Back way."

Zendt jerked a thumb over his shoulder. "End of that hall. Good luck." He stuck out his hand. I took it hastily and brought mine away with a business card folded in it.

The detectives were bumping into desks and cursing behind me when I made the end of the hall and sprinted out the back door. I ran around the building to my car. One of the cops, graying with a thick mustache, had doubled back and was barreling out the front door when I got under the wheel. I scratched pavement with the car door flapping. In the mirror I saw him draw his revolver and sight down on the car. I went into a swerve, but his partner reached him then and knocked up his elbow. I was four blocks away before I heard their siren.

I backed the car into a deserted driveway and unfolded the card Zendt had given me. It was engraved with George Strong's name, telephone number, and address on Lake Shore Drive in Grosse Pointe Farms. I waited a little. When I was sure I couldn't hear the siren any more I pulled out. My head stayed sunk between my shoulder blades until I was past the city limits.

It was one of the deep walled estates facing the glass-flat surface of Lake St. Clair, with a driveway that wound through a lawn as big as a golf course, but greener, ending in front of a brownstone sprawl with windows the size of suburbs. I tucked the Chevy in behind a row of German cars and walked around the house toward the pulse of music. I should have packed a lunch.

Rich people aren't always throwing parties; it's just that that's the only time you catch them at home. This one was going on around a wallet-shaped pool with guests in bathing suits and designer-original sundresses and ascots and silk blazers. There was a small band, not more than sixteen pieces, and the partygoers outnumbered the serving staff by a good one and a half to one.

George Strong wasn't hard to spot. He had made his fortune from newspapers and cable television, and his employees had dutifully smeared his face all over the pages and airwaves during two unsuccessful campaigns for state office. His tow head and crinkled bronze face towered four inches over his tallest listener in a knot of people standing by the rosebushes. I inserted some polyester into the group and introduced myself.

"Do we know each other?" Strong looked older in person than in his ads. His chin sagged and his face was starting to bloat.

"It's about one of your reporters, Ed Stillwell."

"I heard. Terrible thing. The company will pay his bills, even though the incident had nothing to do with the newspaper. I understand he was drunk when they mugged him."

"Nobody mugged him. I think he was beaten by the police."

"Excuse us, gentlemen." He put a hand on my arm and steered me toward the house.

His study was all dark oak and red leather with rows of un-
read books on shelves and photographs of George Strong
shaking hands with governors and presidents. When we were
on opposite sides of an Empire desk I told him the story. Un-
consciously he patted the loosening flesh under his chin.

"Ridiculous. The police in Iroquois Heights aren't thugs."

"Two of them tried to arrest me for Stillwell's beating in
the *Spectator* office half an hour ago, without a warrant.
They followed me there from my house, where they have no
jurisdiction. Your classifieds editor gave me your card. Call
him."

He didn't. "I won't have my reporters manhandled. You say
you want to go through Stillwell's desk?"

I said yes. He took a sheet of heavy stock out of a drawer
and scribbled on it with a gold pen from an onyx stand. He
folded it and handed it to me. "I'll pay double what the woman's paying you to forget the dog and find out who beat up
Stillwell."

"Save it for your next campaign. If my hunch is right I'll
find them both in the same spot." I put the note in my pocket
and took myself out.

The navy blue Chrysler was parked across the street from
the newspaper office when I came around the corner from
where I'd left my car. There was only one man in it, which
meant his partner was watching the back door. I ducked inside
a department store down the block to think.

There was a fire exit in Men's Wear with a warning sign in
red. The clerk, slim and black in a gray three-piece, was helping a customer pick out a necktie by the dressing rooms. I
pushed through the door.

The alarm was good and loud. Mustache had gotten out of
the car and was hustling through the front door when I
rounded the building and trotted across the street to the *Spectator*. The skinny woman in the tailored suit read Strong's note
and pointed out Ed Stillwell's desk.

Reporters are packrats. While I was sifting through a ton of
scrawled-over scrap, Rube Zendt came over and leaned on the
desk. "Cops are watching the place," he said.

"Do tell."

"The older one with the mustache is Sergeant Gogol. The wrestler's Officer Joyce. They're meaner than two vice principals. When you're ready to go, hide in the toilet and I'll call in Joyce from the back—tell him Gogol's got you out front or something—and you can duck out the rear. It worked once."

"I guess you scribblers look out for each other."

"Stillwell? Can't stand the bald son of a bitch. But ink's thicker than blood." He strolled back to his desk.

Ten minutes later I found something that looked good, one half of a fifty dollar bill with a scrap of paper clipped to it and "9 P.M. 8/8 OHS" penciled on the scrap in Stillwell's crooked hand. Today was the eighth. The torn-bill gag was corny as anything, but that was Iroquois Heights for you. I pocketed it, got Zendt's attention, and went to the bathroom.

I spent the rest of the day in a Detroit motel in case the cops went to my house or office. From there I called Elda Chase to tell her I was still working and to ask if she'd heard anything. She hadn't. I watched TV, ordered a pizza for dinner, and left three slices for the maid at eight thirty.

The old high school was lit up like Homecoming when I presented myself at the open front door. A security guard in khaki asked me if I was there for the parents' meeting. I handed him the half-bill. He looked at it, dug the other half out of a shirt pocket, and matched them. Then he put both halves in the pocket. "You're Stillwell?"

"Yeah."

"I heard you was in the hospital."

"I got out." I passed him ahead of any more questions.

A meeting was going on somewhere in the building; voices droned in the linoleum and tile halls. Acting on instinct I headed away from them, stepping around a folding gate beyond which the overhead lights had been turned off. A new noise reached me: louder, not as stylized, less human. It increased as I passed through twin doors and stopped before a steel one marked BOILER ROOM. I opened it and stepped into tropical heat.

I was on a catwalk overlooking the basement, where twenty

men in undershirts or no shirts at all crouched around fifteen
square feet of bare concrete floor, shouting and shaking their
fists at a pair of pit bulls ripping at each other in the center.
From the pitch of their snarls it was still early in the fight, but
already the floor was patterned with blood.

The door opened behind me while I was leaning over the
pipe railing trying to get a look at the men's faces. I stepped
back behind the door, crowding into a dark corner smelling of
cobwebs and crumbling cement. I wished I'd brought my gun
with me. I'd thought it would slow me down.

Two men came in and stood with their backs to me, close
enough to breathe down their collars. I recognized Henry
Revere's white head and green workclothes. The other man's
hair wasn't much darker. He was taller and white, wearing a
gray summerweight suit cut to disguise an advanced middle-
aged spread. From the back he looked familiar.

"Which dog's that?" wheezed the man in the suit. I knew
that broken windpipe.

"Lord Baltimore," said Revere. "Bart. He's new."

"He doesn't have the weight to start out that hard. He'll fold
in five."

"That's a bull for you. Shepherds pace themselves."

"Shepherds are pansies. I told you not to buy any more."

"I gots to buy something. We're running out of dogs."

"Sell what you got. I'm jumping this racket."

"Man, I don't like the other. That's heat with a big *H*."

"*I'm* the heat."

"What if one of them cons talks to the press?"

The man in the suit coughed. "Why'd he want to? What
other chance he got to miss a stretch in Jackson? He should
thank us."

"Not if he gets beat half to death like that reporter."

"Gogol and Joyce got carried away. They were supposed to
just rough him around, maybe break something. Anyway he
had his slice. He should've stood on his tongue."

"What I mean," Revere said. "If he talked, so could a con.
And what about that detective?"

"I got men everyplace he goes. His wings are clipped."

"You say so, chief. I feel better when he's grounded."

A shrill yelp sheared the air. Then silence.

"There, you see?" said the man in the suit. "No distance."

The door opened again. I squeezed tight to the wall. The pair turned, and I got a good view in profile at Acting Chief of Police Mark Proust's long slack face. His complexion matched the gray of his suit.

"Chief, that guy Stillwell's here. Thought I better tell you." The security man's voice was muffled a little on the other side of the open door.

"Impossible. What'd he look like?"

"About six feet, one eighty-five, brown hair."

"That's not—"

I hit the door with my shoulder, occupying the guard while I shoved Proust into the railing. Revere moved my way, but his short leg slowed him down. I swept past him and threw a right at the guard, missing his jaw but glancing off the muscle on the side of his neck. He lost his balance. I vaulted over him.

"It's Walker!" Proust shouted. "Use your gun!"

Flying through the twin doors in the hall, I sent a late dog rooter sprawling. Behind me a shot flattened the air. The bullet shattered the glass in one of the doors. I reached the folding gate, but the opening was gone; the guard or someone had closed and locked it. The guard was coming through the broken door, behind his gun. I ducked through a square arch in the wall, stumbled on stairs in the darkness, caught my equilibrium on the run, and started taking them two at a time heading up. A bullet skidded off brick next to my right ear.

I ran out of stairs on a dark landing. Feet pounded the steps behind me. I felt for and found a doorknob. It turned.

Cool fresh air slid over me down a shaft of moonlight. I was on the roof with the lights of Iroquois Heights spread at my feet. I let the heavy door slam shut of its own weight, got my bearings, and made for the fire chute. I had a foot over the edge when the security guard piled out the door and skidded to a halt, bringing his gun up in two hands. Gravity took me.

The inside of the tube smelled of stale metal. My ears

roared as I slid a long way, as if falling in a dream. Then I lev
eled out and my feet hit ground and inertia carried me uprigh
and forward. Officer Joyce, standing at the bottom, pivoted hi
bulk and brought his right arm down with a grunt. A fuse blev
in my head and I went down another chute, this one bottom
less.

I awoke with a flash of nausea. My scalp stung and an in
flated balloon was rubbing against the inside of my skull. I go
my eyelids open despite sand in the works, only to find that
was still in darkness. This darkness stank. As I lay waiting fo
my pupils to catch up, I grew aware of an incessant loud yap
ping and that it was not in my head. Then I identified th
smell. I was in a kennel.

Not quite in it, I thought, as objects around me assume
vague shape. I was lying on moist earth surrounded by wir
cages with wet black muzzles pressed against the wire from
inside and eyes shining farther back. These were the quie
ones. The others were setting up a racket and hurling them
selves against the doors and trying to gnaw through th
wire.

My arms had gone to sleep. I tried to move them, and tha
was when I found out my wrists were cuffed behind me. M
ankles were bound, too, with something thin and strong tha
chafed skin; twine or insulated wire. I rolled over onto m
face and worked myself up onto my knees. The balloon insid
my head creaked.

Something rattled, followed by a current of air that sucke
in light. The walls were gray corrugated steel. A pair of shin
black Oxfords appeared in front of me and I looked up a
Mark Proust. The battery-powered lantern he was carryin
shadowed the pouches in his paper-pulp face.

"Cut his legs loose," he said. "He isn't going anywhere."

Feet scraped earth behind me. A blade sawed fiber and m
ankles came apart. I got up awkwardly with my wrists sti
bound. Circulation needled back into my lower legs.

"When was the last time, snoop? The Broderick kill?"

I said nothing. Officer Joyce joined Proust, folding a jack

:nife. The crewcut gave his face a planed look, like a wooden :arving with the features blocked in for finishing later.

"Shut up those dogs," Proust said.

I hadn't realized Henry Revere was present. The old black man came up from behind me and kicked the cage containing he loudest of the dogs. The dog, a sixty pound pit bull, topped barking and shrank back snarling. He kicked two more. The third dog hesitated, then lunged, fangs biting wire. Revere kicked again and it yelped and cowered. Its eyes glit-ered in the shadows at the rear of the cage. The rest of the ani-mals fell into a whimpering silence. Two of the cages :ontained shepherds.

"Know where we are, snoop?" asked Proust.

"The Iroquois Heights Police Academy," I said. "Those are ome of your new rookies."

"Funny guy. It's my little ten-acre retirement nest egg six miles out of the Heights. The old high school's nice, but it's oo close to everything."

"Makes a good front, though," I said. "Like dog fighting, which is illegal but forgivable in case someone starts prying. Maybe he won't think to look further and find the real racket."

"What's that, snoop?"

I said nothing again.

"Smart." He smirked at Joyce and Revere. "A smart private nose is what we got here. Only he just thinks he's smart. Thinks if he acts dumb we'll let him go on breathing. Which makes him dumb for real."

I shrugged. "Okay. I heard enough to know you've gradu-ated from fighting dogs to fighting inmates, probably from downtown holding. In return for their release or a word to the udge they agree to fight each other, probably in front of a crowd that's outgrown betting on dogs. Your piece of the gate must be sweet."

"It pays the bills. Especially when we put a black in the pit with a white. A lot of the residents here left Detroit to get away from the blacks. No offense, Henry."

"I'm surprised you didn't put one in with Stillwell."

"He wouldn't have lasted two minutes. Gogol and Joyce al-

most killed him without even trying." He paused, tasting hi
next words. "I figure you for a better show."

"I was wondering when we were coming to that."

"You might win, who knows?"

"What do I win, a bullet?"

"Warm up if you want. People are still coming. I'll sen
someone back for you." He went out, trailing Joyce and Re
vere. A padlock rattled.

It was a truss barn with a high roof and some moonligh
seeping through cracks between the bolted-on sections. Th
cage doors were latched with simple sliding bolts. I backed u
to them and worked them loose, hoping the agitated dogs in
side wouldn't chew off my fingers. I left them engaged jus
enough to keep the doors closed. A good lunge would slip an
of them. I came to the shepherds last. In the gloom either o
them could have been the dog in the picture Elda Chase ha
given me.

"Max."

One of them barked sharply. I called again. It barked again
The other looked at me and gave a rippling snarl. Just to b
sure. I left both cages locked. They were safer inside.

Some of the cages were empty and I sat on one. I wanted
cigarette but I didn't fidget. The last thing I wanted to do wa
startle a dog into breaking loose while I was still present.

After a long time of measured breathing and sweating be
yond measure, I heard the lock rattle again and Gogol an
Joyce came in. I stood. The detective with the mustache hel
his revolver on me while his partner led me out. Gogol fol
lowed with the gun.

We walked twenty yards through a jumble of cars parked o
rutted earth to a steel barn bigger than the one we had just lef
Henry Revere passed us coming out the door. He was goin
back to see to the dogs.

The interior was lit with electric bulbs strung along the top
of the walls. Crude bleachers had been erected on either sid
of a hole dug five feet deep and eight feet in diameter an
lined with rough concrete. The bleachers were jammed wit
men and some women, all talking in loud voices that grev
shrill when we entered. This building smelled as strong as th

other, but the stink here was sharper, more foul, distinctly human. Proust sat in the middle of the front row.

We stopped at the edge of the pit and Joyce unlocked my handcuffs. Inside the pit stood a black man wearing only faded bluejeans. His hair was cropped short and his torso was slabbed with glistening muscle. He watched me with yellowish eyes under a ridge of bone.

I was rubbing circulation back into my wrists when Joyce shoved me into the pit. My opponent caught me and hurled me backward. I struck concrete, emptying my lungs. The crowd shrieked. He charged. I pivoted just in time to avoid being crushed between him and the wall. He caught himself with his hands, pushed off, and whirled. I hit him with everything, flush on the chin. He shook his head. I threw a left. He caught it in a hand the size of my office and hit me on the side of the head with his other fist. I heard a gong.

I backpedaled, buying time for my vision to clear. He followed me. I kicked him in the groin and punched him in the throat; he was no boxer and had left both unprotected. They didn't need protecting. He wrapped his hand around my neck and reared back. "Sorry, man."

The fist was coming at me when a woman in the crowd screamed. The scream was higher and louder than any of the others and it made him hesitate just an instant.

I didn't. I doubled both fists and brought them up in an uppercut that tipped his head back and snapped his teeth together and broke his grip on my neck. Then I put my head down and butted him in the chest. He staggered back, spitting teeth.

The whole crowd was screaming now, and not at us. A torn and bleeding Henry Revere had stumbled into the building trailing a pack of enraged dogs that were bounding through the audience, bellowing and slashing at limbs and throats with the madness of fear and anger and pain. One, a red-eyed pit bull, leaped over the concrete rim and landed on my dazed opponent and I clubbed it with my forearm before it could rip out his throat. Stunned, the dog sank down on all fours and fouled the pit.

"You all right?" I asked.

He got his feet under him, a hand on his throat. It came away bloody, but the skin was barely torn. "I guess."

"What'd they promise you, a clean ticket?"

"Probation."

"Give me a leg up and maybe you'll still get it."

After a moment he complied and I scrambled out of the pit, then stuck out a hand and helped him out. Most of the crowd had cleared out of the building. One of the dogs lay dead, shot through the head by one of the cops; the report had been drowned in the confusion. Another stood panting and glaze-eyed with its tongue hanging out of a scarlet muzzle. I didn't look for the others. My former opponent and I went out the door.

It was more dangerous outside now than in. Cars were swinging out of the makeshift parking lot, sideswiping one another and raking headlamps over scurrying pedestrians and dogs.

I heard sirens getting nearer. I wondered who had called the cops. I wondered which cops they had called.

A maroon Cadillac swung into the light spilling out the barn door, illuminating Proust's pale face behind the wheel. I shouted at the black man and we ran after it. His legs were longer than mine; he reached the car first and tore open the door on the driver's side and pulled Proust out with one hand. The car kept going and stalled against the corner of the other building.

The black man took a gun from under Proust's coat and hit him with it. I let him, then twisted it out of his grip from behind. His other hand was clutching the acting police chief's collar. Proust was bleeding from a cut on his forehead.

"Police! Freeze! Drop the gun!"

I did both. A county sheriff's car had pulled up alongside us and a deputy was coming out with his gun in both hands. The door on the passenger's side opened and George Strong got out.

"It's all right," he said. "That's our inside man."

The deputy kept his stance. "What about the other?"

I said, "He's with me."

Strong looked from Proust's half-conscious face to mine. "I

bribed the guard at the high school for this spot. I remembered I was a newspaperman and that maybe the biggest story in years was getting away from me. What about the ones who hurt Stillwell?"

"Sergeant Gogol and officer Joyce," I said. "APB them."

His crinkled face got wry. "Did you find the woman's dog?"

I indicated the other barn. "In there. Take it easy on him," I told the deputy. "Take it easy on all of them."

"You a dog lover or something?"

"No, just one of the dogs." I walked away to breathe.

HAMADRYAD

WILLIAM BEECHCROFT

Ten miles north of Fort Myers—where the Tamiami Trail arrowed through miles of scrub and sand and the fringes of Punta Gorda hadn't shown up yet—Sammy "Little Shot" Pippitone pushed himself straighter behind the wheel of his rented Honda Civic. The Garden of Serpents should be coming up soon, according to the info he'd been given yesterday. Out here in the southwest Florida boondocks, he ought to be able to make the hit Q & E—quick and easy—then zip back down to the Southwest Regional and catch a redeye back north in time for an early breakfast in Manhattan.

Sammy's nickname hadn't come from his smallness, though he wasn't a lot bigger than a slightly oversized jockey. They called him "Little Shot" because he was at the bottom end of the caliber scale from Orlo "Big Shot" Orsini. The Big Shot packed one of the new .50-caliber Desert Eagles, a monster hand-cannon with huge, half-inch-diameter Spear Lawman ammo that would stop a charging rhino if there'd been one up in Queens to try it on. It also made a gut-jarring bang you could hear from Borden Avenue all the way up to 44th, even with heavy traffic.

Sammy Little Shot hated Orlo's kind of slam-bang service. Sammy considered himself an artist at what he did. No big boom. He used a sweet little .25-caliber Sterling Model 300, a six-shot automatic only four and a half inches overall—not much more than eight inches with its fat steel carrot of a noise suppressor threaded to its muzzle. Sammy never called the fat carrot a silencer. There was no such thing as a "silencer," but

the suppressor cut the Sterling's normal bark to no more than a
sput. Sammy always placed that little sput just an inch from
the mark's skull, just behind the ear. The neat, quiet work of
an artist.

He'd gotten the Sterling here in the bag he'd checked
through from JFK. The airlines didn't often x-ray checked
baggage. If they did, his bag carried a phony name and address
tag. And he was always careful to case the crowd at baggage
pickup, willing to let the bag stay on the conveyor if he spotted any security waiting. At Southwest Regional, nobody had
looked suspicious about anything. A holiday crowd.

There the place was, maybe a mile ahead on the right, a
one-story, pink stucco building done in phony Spanish hacienda style. Sammy let the speedometer begin to slip back
from sixty-five. The speed limit was fifty-five, but everybody
else was topping that. A cream and brown RV blared past to
his left as he pulled off the road and found a slot in the sand
and crushed-shell parking lot.

Lester Biorkin, the target's name was. Or had been. Now
the Federal Witness Program called him Louis Burke, according to Sammy's briefing phone call yesterday. As far as the
Family was concerned, the FWP was a great help. The Family
had a mole there, and the mole could turn up just about anything they wanted. At the moment, they wanted Biorkin, who
had done three hateful things that upset them. First, a year ago
he had witnessed from his taxi up in Harlem the disposal by
gunshot of Don Dominic Giovanchi. That wouldn't have been
bad if Giovanchi's recycling had been handled by one of the
Family's routine disposers. But the hit had been made personally by Don Edmundo Carli himself. "I owe him that honor,"
Don Carli himself had explained it to his worried security
pros. Anyway, who'd of thought a dumb taxi driver would be
wandering along Lenox Avenue just as Don Carli's .45 bright-
ened the night? Who'd of thought the driver would recognize
the distinguished shooter? But worst of all, who'd of thought
the hack driver would do the second hateful thing: be dumb
enough to testify and put Don Carli himself up the Hudson in
Ossining for twenty-five to thirty-five?

Worse. When word from Don Carli himself came down out

of Sing Sing, a worker shooter named Skagg had been sent to Miami to take care of Biorkin. Dancing through Biscayne Boulevard traffic a couple of feet behind Biorkin, Skagg went under a gravel truck, or so the story went. That was the third hateful thing. Biorkin made it across the highway, but Skagg was roadkill. At that point, the Family decided a worker shooter had been a bad choice, and they contacted a specialist shooter, namely Sammy Little Shot.

Now here Sammy was, sliding one slender, polished black Thom McAn out of the Honda to the dusty parking surface, then the other. Wrong shoes, he knew, but he hadn't had much time to put his wardrobe together for this little swing south. It had been "Five Gs and leave now, or be picky, wait for the next one, and hope you don't starve in between." Nice way the Family had of putting things. So here he was. The blue and white seersucker pants would be okay, the button-down white shirt would pass. The blue poplin jacket was already too hot, but he couldn't take it off because that would expose the hand-grip of the Sterling stuck in his waistband.

He left the car unlocked in case he'd need to make a speedy exit, shaded his eyes, and looked up at the facade of the Spanish hacienda. And that was when he felt icy slivers prickle his spine. All through the plane trip down to Fort Myers then back up here by Japanese scooter, he had pushed to the back of his brain just where he had to go to find Biorkin-Burke. The Garden of Serpents was a tourist attraction, a goddamned snakearium, and if there was anything he hated enough to send cold slivers up his arms just by thinking about it, it was a snake. Hated them even worse than bats, and he hated bats enough to try to stay inside after dark—even in Midtown in winter. The bat hate had come from his mother, when he'd been a kid back in Jersey City. One had gotten into her bedroom and she'd gone bonkers, rolling on the floor, screaming it was going to get in her hair and strangle her. When he was older, he knew that probably wouldn't have happened, but it never stopped giving him the shakes. Even now, he couldn't make it all the way through a Dracula movie.

The snake business had started when he was ten. He and a buddy had chased a grass snake under a fence. The buddy ran

around the other side, screamed, "I got it!" and stepped on it
just as Sammy leaned down with his mouth open. Something
green and sour and vile squirted out of the snake's mouth
straight into his. He spit and gagged and spit and thought he
was going to die.

As Sammy stared up at the big green and pink lettering
across the whole front of the Garden of Serpents, he felt that
old gagging urge begin to throb in his throat. The letters were
decorated with vines—until a second look showed him the
vines were snakes, holding each other's tails in their mouths.
The sun, low on the horizon behind him, made the entwined
lettering seem to writhe in its brassy glare. He swallowed his
revulsion and walked into the building.

A few tourists fingered the gaudy souvenir racks that
flanked a sales counter on the left side of the tiled lobby. On
the right were a pair of restroom doors labeled "Hiss" and
"Herss." the entrance to the exhibits was center rear, a heavy
solid wood door with a ticket cage just to its left.

He realized he was stalling, hoping that somehow Biorkin
would magically appear, walk out to the parking lot, and make
things easy. Sammy didn't want to go in there. But Biorkin
worked here. He had to be out there doing something or other
in the exhibit area. To avoid the guy's leaving through a back
door while he stood there wondering about it, Sammy had to
make himself go in there. He yanked out his wallet, careful not
to expose the gun butt, and handed the five-buck tariff to the
bored-looking babe behind the screened ticket window. Then
he faced the big, curved-top entrance, took a long, deep
breath, and pulled it open.

Years ago he'd read that snakes smell like cucumbers. That
might have been a lot of horse hocky, but he could swear that
as he stepped through the door, all of a sudden he smelled cucumbers. And there wasn't a snake in sight. He'd expected a
big room with cages along the wall. It wasn't like that at all.
He walked across a sort of hallway, then he was outdoors
again, in a big courtyard open to the darkening sky. The central
area was crisscrossed by two brick walks at right angles. The
walks intersected in the middle, cutting the yard into four sections. In each section was a—what? Some kind of cinderblock

ring. Sammy walked over to the nearest one, his shoes scuff
ing the tanbark mulch. He peered into the big fifteen-foot
diameter well. His blood turned to instant ice. Down there i
the bottom of the six-foot-deep pit was a writhing tangle of fa
black snakes. Christ, there must be a hundred of them, Samm
realized.

He stumbled backwards until his feet found brick again. A
wave of black dots threatened to black out his vision. He
fought it off. Okay. He was okay now. But he sure didn't wan
to see what was in the other three wells.

The roofed hallway that ran around all four sides of the
courtyard was formed by a wall without windows all around
the outside, and a low parapet sort of wall around the inside
Widely spaced concrete columns jutted up from the parapet to
support the roof's inside edge. All along the outside wall o
this open hallway Sammy made out rows of glass cages. He
was glad the light was getting so bad he couldn't see what wa
in them.

In a distant corner, a knot of people had gathered around
some guy in a white coat. Sammy couldn't spot anybody any
where else in here, so he walked across the courtyard toward
the gathering. He was careful not to throw any careless look
into the two wells he passed on the way.

Standing at the edge of the little crowd down here in the
corner, he could see that the short guy in the white coat wa
working with something on the edge of the parapet. A citize
with ape shoulders moved aside and Sammy saw what wa
going on. The white-coat guy had a damned snake right ou
here with everybody. Only his little pole with a hook at the
end was between him and the snake.

Sammy was surprised that he knew what kind of snake i
was. The flaring hood was a dead giveaway. This skinny little
snake man with brushcut gray hair was diddling around with a
cobra. A couple of feet of cobra, and the lousy cobra was get
ting tired of it. It made a lunge for the guy's hand. Just as i
did, the guy whipped in with the other hand, and Sammy wa
goggle-eyed. The bony little snake charmer had the thing by
the back of its neck.

"You going to show us the hamadryad this afternoon, Dr.

Grosvenor?" The speaker was a brainy-looking teenager crowding right in on the cobra act.

"Afraid not, son." The snake doctor had a voice as dry as scales on leaves. "We bring him out only on Sundays."

Sammy wondered vaguely what in hell a "hammer dry head" was, but his attention came back to the matter at hand in a hurry. From the shadows behind the parapet an arm reached out to give the snake wrestler a glass flask with rubber stretched across its mouth. The guy with a handful of cobra brought the flask up to the snake, and it zapped its fangs deep in the rubber top. Sammy was revolted, but he couldn't make himself look away as the yellowish venom drooled down the inside of the glass. The snake's glittery little eyes looked like he was having a fine old time sinking his fangs into something.

Then Sammy shook his head to break the tight little string of horror that had tied him to the cobra. And he got a look at the guy who'd handed out the flask.

He was tall, with neatly styled black hair and sharp green eyes in the kind of face Sammy had seen as mercenary of the month on *Soldiers for Hire* magazine. Just the kind of good-looking, overconfident guy Sammy liked to whack. "Gives me a lot of satisfaction," he had relayed back to Don Carli up there in 'Sing. What he didn't say, but knew was true, was that whacking a guy like Biorkin here made up some for Sammy's being so little that everybody was always looking down at the top of his head.

While the spidery snake doctor went on with his show for the tourist trade, Sammy edged over to the parapet where the glass-flask supply ace was idling now that he'd had his big moment. Yeah, this was sure as hell who he'd come here for. Sammy recognized him from the photo the Family had thoughtfully provided.

He felt so good about it, so pleased at the way this was working out, that he smiled at the target and said quietly, "Hi, Biorkin." Call it bravado or whatever, it was his trademark. The murmured greeting with a big smile just before the whack. It confused them, and a confused target was an easy target.

Biorkin didn't react at all. Maybe he hadn't even heard him.
Too bad. For Sammy the edge was gone now, and the rest of
this would be nothing more than mechanics.

Dr. Brushcut was folding up his act now, and Sammy
stayed on the fringe of the crowd as it ambled to the big courtyard door. Near the door, though, he drifted off to the left,
then fitted himself neatly behind the roof column in the southwest corner of the yard.

Everybody was out of the place now except for the snake
charmer and Biorkin, who was obviously his assistant. Having
the two of them in here made things dicey. Then Sammy heard
the doc call out, "Good night, Lou," and he made out the little
snaker walking up the hallway on the other side of the courtyard. The light was getting really bad now. The guy turned the
corner and came straight down the west hall toward Sammy.
But, as Sammy had figured, the snake doctor stopped at the
main door, pushed it open, and stepped out of the exhibit yard
into the lobby.

This was beautiful, Sammy realized. Only he and "Lou"
Biorkin were left in here. Couldn't have engineered a better
setup if he'd planned it.

He listened. The courtyard was dead silent. Had Biorkin
somehow slipped out with the crowd? Or maybe out the back?
Sammy racked his memory. Was there a back door down
there?

Then he heard a rattle. A rattle!! Come on, calm down, he
ordered himself. Rattlesnakes don't make door noises. There
was a door back there, and son of a bitch Biorkin was going
through it!

Sammy sprinted down the south hallway, first running flat
out, then getting a lot more careful as he realized he was ramming along only a foot from the snake cages that lined the outside wall.

He skittered around the southeast corner of the corridor,
raced along the east side, and—hell, here it was, a rear door.
He shoved down the panic bar. The door wouldn't budge. It
was locked by a key-operated deadbolt. Biorkin had gone out
this way, now Sammy had to run all the way back to the main
entrance and—

Wait a minute! What was that? He turned toward the courtyard and listened. Footsteps. Sounded like they were going up
the north corridor toward the door. The guy was still in here!
He'd locked this rear door from the inside, and he was still in
here.

Then Sammy heard the stealthy footsteps pause. There
was a grating noise, like wood sliding on concrete, and Biorkin's padding steps picked up again, heading for the main entrance.

Sammy launched himself straight up the middle of the
courtyard. Biorkin was still over on the north side, and if
Sammy was quick enough, he could reach the main door the
same time Biorkin did.

At the midpoint, where the two walkways intersected, Sammy's leather-soled shoes slipped. He went down on one knee,
cracking it painfully against the bricks. He'd told himself he
ought to start wearing rubber soles, but he hadn't found a pair
that looked decent. He was up again almost as soon as he'd
gone down, but the slip had cost him. He caught a dim
glimpse of Biorkin's white coat as the big main door opened, a
flash of the lobby lighting, then the door slammed shut again.

Biorkin was in the lobby, no doubt racing for his car. Now
Sammy would have to go out there, get in his own car, tail him
until he pulled into his driveway or stopped at some store on
the way home, and improvise from there. This thing was getting more complicated than Sammy liked. He reached the end
of the main walkway and lunged for the door.

Locked. He shook the handle. Locked with a keyed deadbolt like the door behind him.

This was crazy. Him, Sammy Little Shot Pippitone, the
world's greatest snake hater, locked in with a world-class
snake population. He sagged against the door, pulled great
ragged breaths, and tried not to go into giggle-sob hysterics.
Wait till Big Shot Orsini heard about this! There'd be no end
to the ragging Sammy'd have to take.

He tried to concentrate on that funny side of it, but there
was no getting around what was going on here. He had let a
dumb-ass taxi jock outflank him and lock him in here with
hundreds of—

A hot needle of panic speared through Sammy's tumblin brain. He banged on the door with both fists. "Let me out here! I'm locked in. Let me OUT!"

He put his ear to the door. Nothing. Biorkin must have bee the last person in the place, and now he was gone. Samm slowly turned and faced the courtyard. Silence. Silence blar keted by darkness thick as a quilt. He could barely make ov the rim of the courtyard wall against the overcast, starles night. To his right, almost at his elbow, it seemed, he heard th faint jitter of scales against something dry. A snake over ther was shifting around in his cage. An icy tremor skittered dow Sammy's back.

A flicker of dim blue light silhouetted the east wall of th courtyard. What could— Then distant thunder rumbled. H felt it more than heard it, felt it through the thin soles of hi city Thom McAns. Did the snakes feel it, too? All around hin he heard rustlings and twitchings.

He didn't belong here, for Chrissake! Not here in snak city, Florida, ten miles from nowhere.

Out on the Tamiami Trail, a truck howled past. There wer people going by not a hundred yards away, but he might a well be on the moon.

Come on, Sammy, think. He backed tight against the doo At least this way nothing could sneak up behind him. Clim out of here, maybe? The only access to the roof over th perimeter hallway was up one of the supporting columns. I they'd been narrow enough to get a grip around, he migh have been able to shinny up to the roof. But the columns wer too thick for that.

Lightning flickered again. The seconds between flash an rumble were fewer. Damned storm was getting closer. Like h needed that on top of all his immediate problems.

Slow down, Sammy, he urged himself. There were only tw problems: get out of here, then whack Biorkin. He wasn't to worried about the Biorkin part. He had a line on where the gu lived, and the Family had feelers everywhere in case Biorki skipped. Like he had in Miami. The big problem was righ now: getting out of this hell hole before he went . . . batty.

He would have to think of that! And this was worse tha

Dracula's castle. There you only had to worry about the count. Here he was surrounded by hundreds of creepy fang-bearers. The image of the cobra biting into the rubber-topped bottle flashed vividly to mind. How could the snake doctor get himself to even *touch* the damned cobra? How many cobras were in here with him? What was in the other three wells? Did the snakes out there crawl out of their pits at night and—

Jesus, what was *that!*

Somewhere over to his left, he'd heard a grating noise, loud and long, like somebody pulling a fire hose around a corner. *That* sure hadn't been a snake in a cage. It was right out here in the—

Forked lightning flared overhead, strobed the courtyard white. Seconds after darkness fell back in, he could still see it burned in his eyeballs. Empty, thank God, the walkways making a giant cross.

That'd keep old Dracula away, he thought inanely. Then thunder exploded like a ton of TNT going off.

His ears sizzled from the blast. No, that wasn't his ears. It was a hiss. He had definitely heard a hiss. And damned close. Just to his left.

He was *out* of here!

As Sammy leaped into the empty courtyard, he felt something hit his right knee. Then his left shoulder. Soft impacts, but terrifying. Then his face was struck, and he almost laughed through his fright. Raindrops, that's what was hitting him. Nothing but big, fat raindrops.

He stumbled to the center of the courtyard as the scattered drops became a downpour. Then a deluge. The cascading sheets were shot through the jagged spears of lightning that threw the walkways and the concrete-ringed serpent wells into brilliance that blinded him for seconds afterward.

Hunched against the storm's beating downpour, squinting into its lightning flares, soaked and shivering, Sammy shoved his right hand under his sopping jacket and jerked out the Sterling automatic. He was sure now that something was loose here, something more terrifying than anything he'd seen in the cages. He didn't know what it was, didn't even want to imagine, but he knew it was here because he could *feel* it, just like he would have felt a hidden shooter from the rival Giovanchi Family.

But there was something worse than a Giovanchi shooter in here, something that made the hairs on his neck stand straight out. With the pistol held in both hands, Sammy crouched, swung around wildly in the inky blackness. What could—

Lightning strobed twice, only a fraction of a second each time, but it etched into Sammy's retinas a sight so incredible, so terrifying, that Sammy froze tight.

The thing stood taller than Sammy in his shooting crouch. It swayed there, ghostly white with gleaming eyes that stared down at Sammy as hard and merciless as bronze chips.

Dracula! Sammy thought wildly. The crossed sidewalks didn't mean a thing. For a frozen moment, he crouched motionless, praying that what he'd seen had been an illusion, a figment of panic.

Then his stunned brain jerked back on track and he pulled the trigger. He got off just one wild shot as the hellish apparition crashed in over his extended arms and sank daggers into his neck.

"Found him just like that," Doctor of Herpetology Herman Grosvenor told Charlotte County Sheriff Duncan Bosworth. They stood in the center of the courtyard, flanking the body of the little man in the sodden poplin jacket and seersucker trousers; the little man with two widely spaced, bloody punctures in his neck. Nearby, two more men in county sheriff's uniforms were supposed to be checking for "clues," but mostly they stared into the snake wells with obvious distaste.

"And the hama-whatever, you say you found him out of his cage?" Sheriff Bosworth was a big man with a florid face, but Grosvenor could see that under the lacework of beer-bloated capillaries, the sheriff was pale as paste.

"Hamadryad," Dr. Grosvenor amended. "When I got here, I found him footloose and fancy free." He looked down at the body. "I don't know who this unfortunate fellow is, or how he got locked in here. Found him just like this when I opened up this morning."

"Who was the last one to leave last night?" the sheriff asked as he crouched and kind of aimlessly fingered the deceased's neck.

"My assistant, Lou Burke. Oh, you mean, could he have left the cage open? Not him, he's a detail man. It's more likely this fellow came in a misguided effort to steal the hamadryad and it got out of hand."

"The thing's worth money?"

"Well up in five figures, Sheriff." Dr. Grosvenor frowned. "Funny thing about Lou, though. He called in just after I called you, said an emergency had come up, and he had to quit."

The sheriff looked up from his crouch. "Quit?"

"As of today. Said he'd be back in touch to tell me where to send his severance check."

"I'll check on him, but I can't say I blame anybody for giving up this kind of showbiz." Bosworth stood and gazed uneasily around the courtyard. "You're sure you corralled that mama-whatever?"

"Hamadryad, Sheriff. Our king cobra. I can't imagine how he got loose, but he's safely back in his cage. All eighteen feet of him."

"That's some hell of a snake!"

Dr. Grosvenor smiled like a proud parent. "The only snake, I like to say, that can rear up and look you straight in the eye."

THE ORACLE OF THE DOG

G. K. CHESTERTON

"Yes," said Father Brown, "I always like a dog, so long as he isn't spelt backwards."

Those who are quick in talking are not always quick in listening. Sometimes even their brilliancy produces a sort of stupidity. Father Brown's friend and companion was a young man with a stream of ideas and stories, an enthusiastic young man named Fiennes, with eager blue eyes and blond hair that seemed to be brushed back, not merely with a hairbrush but with the wind of the world as he rushed through it. But he stopped in the torrent of his talk in a momentary bewilderment before he saw the priest's very simple meaning.

"You mean that people make too much of them?" he said. "Well, I don't know. They're marvelous creatures. Sometimes I think they know a lot more than we do."

Father Brown said nothing, but continued to stroke the head of the big retriever in a half-abstracted but apparently soothing fashion.

"Why," said Fiennes, warming again to his monologue, "there was a dog in the case I've come to see you about: what they call the 'Invisible Murder Case,' you know. It's a strange story, but from my point of view the dog is about the strangest thing in it. Of course, there's the mystery of the crime itself, and how old Druce can have been killed by somebody else when he was all alone in the summerhouse—"

The hand stroking the dog stopped for a moment in its rhythmic movement, and Father Brown said calmly: "Oh, it was a summerhouse, was it?"

"I thought you'd read all about it in the papers," answered Fiennes. "Stop a minute; I believe I've got a cutting that will give you all the particulars." He produced a strip of newspaper from his pocket and handed it to the priest, who began to read it, holding it close to his blinking eyes with one hand while the other continued its half-conscious caresses of the dog. It looked like the parable of a man not letting his right hand know what his left hand did.

Many mystery stories, about men murdered behind locked doors and windows, and murderers escaping without means of entrance and exit, have come true in the course of the extraordinary events at Cranston on the coast of Yorkshire, where Colonel Druce was found stabbed from behind by a dagger that has entirely disappeared from the scene, and apparently even from the neighborhood.

The summerhouse in which he died was indeed accessible at one entrance, the ordinary doorway which looked down the central walk of the garden, toward the house. But, by a combination of events almost to be called a coincidence, it appears that both the path and the entrance were watched during the crucial time, and there is a chain of witnesses who confirm each other. The summerhouse stands at the extreme end of the garden, where there is no exit or entrance of any kind. The central garden path is a lane between two ranks of tall delphiniums, planted so close that any stray step off the path would leave its traces; and both path and plants run right up to the very mouth of the summerhouse, so that no straying from that straight path could fail to be observed, and no other mode of entrance can be imagined.

Patrick Floyd, secretary of the murdered man, testified that he had been in a position to overlook the whole garden from the time when Colonel Druce last appeared alive in the doorway to the time when he was found dead; as he, Floyd, had been on the top of a stepladder clipping the garden hedge. Janet Druce, the dead man's daughter, confirmed this, saying that she had sat on the terrace of the house throughout that time and had seen Floyd at his work. Touching some part of the time, this is again supported by Donald Druce, her brother—who overlooked the garden—standing at his bedroom window in his dressing gown, for he had risen late. Lastly, the account is consistent with that given by Dr. Valentine, a neighbor, who called for a time to talk with Miss Druce on the terrace, and by the colonel's solicitor, Mr. Aubrey Traill, who was apparently the last to see the murdered man alive—presumably with the exception of the murderer.

All are agreed that the course of events was as follows: About half past three in the afternoon, Miss Druce went down the path to ask her father when he would like tea; but he said he did not want any and was waiting to see Traill, his lawyer, who was to be sent to him in the summerhouse. The girl then came away and met Traill coming down the path; she directed him to her father and he went in as directed. About half an hour afterwards he came out again, the colonel coming with him to the door and showing himself to all appearance in health and even high spirits. He had been somewhat annoyed earlier in the day by his son's irregular hours, but seemed to recover his temper in a perfectly normal fashion, and had been rather markedly genial in receiving other visitors, including two of his nephews, who came over for the day. But as these were out walking during the whole period of the tragedy, they had no evidence to give. It is said, indeed, that the colonel was not on very good terms with Dr. Valentine, but that gentleman only had a brief interview with the daughter of the house, to whom he is supposed to be paying serious attentions.

Traill, the solicitor, says he left the colonel entirely alone in the summerhouse, and this is confirmed by Floyd's bird's-eye view of the garden, which showed nobody else passing the only entrance. Ten minutes later, Miss Druce again went down the garden and had

not reached the end of the path when she saw her fa-
ther, who was conspicuous by his white linen coat,
lying in a heap on the floor. She uttered a scream
which brought others to the spot, and on entering the
place they found the colonel lying dead beside his bas-
ket chair, which was also upset. Dr. Valentine, who
was still in the immediate neighborhood, testified that
the wound was made by some sort of stiletto, entering
under the shoulderblade and piercing the heart. The
police have searched the neighborhood for such a
weapon, but no trace of it can be found.

"So Colonel Druce wore a white coat, did he?" said Father
Brown as he put down the paper.

"Trick he learnt in the tropics," replied Fiennes, with some
wonder. "He'd had some queer adventures there, by his own
account; and I fancy his dislike of Valentine was connected
with the doctor coming from the tropics, too. But it's all an in-
ternal puzzle. The account there is pretty accurate; I didn't see
the tragedy, in the sense of the discovery; I was out walking
with the young nephews and the dog—the dog I wanted to tell
you about. But I saw the stage set for it as described; the
straight line between the blue flowers right up to the dark entrance, and the lawyer going down it in his blacks and his silk
hat, and the red head of the secretary showing high above the
green hedge as he worked on it with his shears. Nobody could
have mistaken that red head at any distance; and if people say
they saw it there all the time, you may be sure they did. This
redhaired secretary, Floyd, is quite a character; a breathless,
bounding sort of fellow, always doing everybody's work as he
was doing the gardener's. I think he is an American; he's certainly got the American view of life—what they call the view-
point, bless 'em."

"What about the lawyer?" asked Father Brown.

There was silence and then Fiennes spoke quite slowly for
him. "Traill struck me as a singular man. In his fine black
clothes he was almost foppish, yet you can hardly call him
fashionable. For he wore a pair of long, luxuriant black
whiskers such as haven't been seen since Victorian times. He

had rather a fine grave face and a fine grave manner, but ever
now and then he seemed to remember to smile. And when h
showed his white teeth he seemed to lose a little of his dignit\
and there was something faintly fawning about him. It ma\
have been only embarrassment, for he would also fidget wit
his cravat and his tie pin, which were at once handsome an
unusual, like himself. If I could think of anybody—but what'
the good, when the whole thing's impossible? Nobody know
who did it. Nobody knows how it could be done. At lea:
there's only one exception I'd make, and that's why I reall\
mentioned the whole thing. The dog knows."

Father Brown sighed and then said absently: "You we\
there as a friend of young Donald, weren't you? He didn't g
on your walk with you?"

"No," replied Fiennes, smiling. "The young scoundrel ha
gone to bed that morning and got up that afternoon. I we\
with his cousins, two young officers from India, and our cor
versation was trivial enough. I remember the elder, whos
name I think is Herbert Druce and who is an authority o
horsebreeding, talked about nothing but a mare he had bougl
and the moral character of the man who sold her; while hi
brother Harry seemed to be brooding on his bad luck at Mon\
Carlo. I only mention it to show you, in the light of what ha\
pened on our walk, that there was nothing psychic about u.
The dog was the only mystic in our company."

"What sort of a dog was he?" asked the priest.

"Same breed as that one," answered Fiennes. "That's wha
started me off on the story, your saying you didn't believe i
believing in a dog. He's a big black retriever, named Nox, an
a suggestive name, too, for I think what he did a darker mys
tery than the murder. You know Druce's house and garden ar
by the sea; we walked about a mile from it along the sands an
then turned back, going the other way. We passed a rather cu
rious rock called the Rock of Fortune, famous in the neighbor
hood because it's one of those examples of one stone barel\
balanced on another, so that a touch would knock it over. It i
not really very high but the hanging outline of it makes it loo
a little wild and sinister; at least it made it look so to me, for
don't imagine my jolly young companions were afflicted wit

the picturesque. But it may be that I was beginning to feel an atmosphere; for just then the question arose of whether it was time to go back to tea, and even then I think I had a premonition that time counted for a good deal in the business. Neither Herbert Druce nor I had a watch, so we called out to his brother, who was some paces behind, having stopped to light his pipe under the hedge. Hence it happened that he shouted out the hour, which was twenty past four, in his big voice through the growing twilight; and somehow the loudness of it made it sound like the proclamation of something tremendous. His unconsciousness seemed to make it all the more so; but that was always the way with omens; and particular ticks of the clock were really very ominous things that afternoon. According to Dr. Valentine's testimony, poor Druce had actually died just about half past four.

"Well, they said we needn't go home for ten minutes, and we walked a little farther along the sands, doing nothing in particular—throwing stones for the dog and throwing sticks into the sea for him to swim after. But to me the twilight seemed to grow oddly oppressive, and the very shadow of the top-heavy Rock of Fortune lay on me like a load. And then the curious thing happened. Nox had just brought back Herbert's walking stick out of the sea and his brother had thrown his in also. The dog swam out again, but just about what must have been the stroke of the half hour, he stopped swimming. He came back again onto the shore and stood in front of us. Then he suddenly threw up his head and sent up a howl or wail of woe—if ever I heard one in the world.

" 'What the devil's the matter with the dog?' asked Herbert; but none of us could answer. There was a long silence after the brute's wailing and whining died away on the desolate shore; and then the silence was broken. As I live, it was broken by a faint and faroff shriek, like the shriek of a woman from beyond the hedges inland. We didn't know what it was then; but we knew afterwards. It was the cry the girl gave when she first saw the body of her father."

"You went back, I suppose," said Father Brown patiently. "What happened then?"

"I'll tell you what happened then," said Fiennes with a grim

emphasis. "When we got back into that garden, the first thing
we saw was Traill, the lawyer; I can see him now with his
black hat and black whiskers relieved against the perspective
of the blue flowers stretching down to the summerhouse, with
the sunset and the strange outline of the Rock of Fortune in the
distance. His face and figure were in shadow against the sunset; but I swear the white teeth were showing in his head and
he was smiling.

"The moment Nox saw that man, the dog dashed forward
and stood in the middle of the path barking at him madly, mur-
derously, volleying out curses that were almost verbal in their
dreadful distinctness of hatred. And the man doubled up and
fled along the path between the flowers."

Father Brown sprang to his feet with a startling impatience.

"So the dog denounced him, did he?" he cried. "The oracle
of the dog condemned him. Did you see what birds were flying, and are you sure whether they were on the right hand or
the left? Did you consult the augurs about the sacrifices?
Surely you didn't omit to cut open the dog and examine his
entrails. That is the sort of scientific test you heathen humani-
tarians seem to trust when you are thinking of taking away the
life and honor of man."

Fiennes sat gaping for an instant before he found breath to
say: "Why, what's the matter with you? What have I done
now?"

A sort of anxiety came back into the priest's eyes—the anxiety of a man who has run against a post in the dark and won-
ders for a moment whether he has hurt it.

"I'm most awfully sorry," he said with sincere distress. "I
beg your pardon for being so rude; pray forgive me."

Fiennes looked at him curiously. "I sometimes think you are
more of a mystery than any of the mysteries," he said. "But
anyhow, if you don't believe in the mystery of the dog, at least
you can't get over the mystery of the man. You can't deny that
at the very moment when the beast came back from the sea
and bellowed, his master's soul was driven out of his body by
the blow of some unseen power that no mortal man can trace
or even imagine. And as for the lawyer—I don't go only by
the dog—there are other curious details, too. He struck me as a

smooth, smiling, equivocal sort of person; and one of his tricks seemed like a sort of hint. You know the doctor and the police were on the spot very quickly; Valentine was brought back when walking away from the house, and he telephoned instantly. That, with the secluded house, small numbers, and enclosed space, made it pretty possible to search everybody who could have been near; and everybody was thoroughly searched—for a weapon. The whole house, garden, and shore were combed for a weapon. The disappearance of the dagger is almost as crazy as the disappearance of the man."

"The disappearance of the dagger," said Father Brown, nodding. He seemed to have become suddenly attentive.

"Well," continued Fiennes, "I told you that man Traill had a trick of fidgeting with his tie and tie pin—especially his tie pin. His pin, like himself, was at once showy and old fashioned. It had one of those stones with concentric colored rings that look like an eye; and his own concentration on it got on my nerves, as if he had been a Cyclops with one eye in the middle of his body. But the pin was not only large but long; and it occurred to me that his anxiety about its adjustment was because it was even longer than it looked; as long as a stiletto in fact."

Father Brown nodded thoughtfully. "Was any other instrument ever suggested?" he said.

"There was another suggestion," answered Fiennes, "from one of the young Druces—the cousins, I mean. Neither Herbert nor Harry Druce would have struck one at first as likely to be of assistance in scientific detection; but while Herbert was really the traditional type of heavy dragoon, caring for nothing but horses and being an ornament to the Horse Guards, his younger brother Harry had been in the Indian police and knew something about such things. Indeed, in his own way he was quite clever; and I rather fancy he had been too clever; I mean he had left the police through breaking some red tape regulations and taking some sort of risk and responsibility of his own. Anyhow, he was in some sense a detective out of work, and threw himself into this business with more than the ardor of an amateur. And it was with him that I had an argument about the weapon—an argument that led to something new. It

began by his countering my description of the dog barking a
Traill; and he said that a dog at his worst didn't bark, bu
growled."

"He was quite right there," observed the priest.

"This young fellow went on to say that, if it came to tha
he'd heard Nox growling at other people before then; an
among others at Floyd, the secretary. I retorted that his ow
argument answered itself; for the crime couldn't be brough
home to two or three people, and least of all to Floyd, wh
was as innocent as a harum-scarum schoolboy, and had bee
seen by everybody all the time perched above the garde
hedge with his fan of red hair as conspicuous as a scarlet cock
atoo. "I know there's difficulties anyhow," said my colleague
"but I wish you'd come with me down the garden a minute.
want to show you something I don't think anyone else ha
seen." This was on the very day of the discovery, and the gar
den was just as it had been. The stepladder was still standin
by the hedge, and just under the hedge my guide stopped an
disentangled something from the deep grass. It was the shear
used for clipping the hedge, and on the point of one of them
was a smear of blood."

There was a short silence, and then Father Brown said sud
denly, "What was the lawyer there for?"

"He told us the colonel sent for him to alter his will," an
swered Fiennes. "And, by the way, there was another thin;
about the business of the will that I ought to mention. You see
the will wasn't actually signed in the summerhouse that after
noon."

"I suppose not," said Father Brown; "there would have to b
two witnesses."

"The lawyer actually came down the day before and it wa
signed then; but he was sent for again next day because the ol
man had a doubt about one of the witnesses and had to be re
assured."

"Who were the witnesses?" asked Father Brown.

"That's just the point," replied his informant eagerly, "th
witnesses were Floyd, the secretary, and this Dr. Valentine
the foreign sort of surgeon or whatever he is; and the two ha
a quarrel. Now, I'm bound to say that the secretary is some

thing of a busybody. He's one of those hot and headlong people whose warmth of temperament has unfortunately turned mostly to pugnacity and bristling suspicion; to distrusting people instead of to trusting them. That sort of redhaired red-hot fellow is always either universally credulous or universally incredulous; and sometimes both. He was not only a jack-of-all-trades, but he knew better than all tradesmen. He not only knew everything, but he warned everybody against everybody. All that must be taken into account in his suspicions about Valentine; but in that particular case there seems to have been something behind it. He said the name of Valentine was not really Valentine. He said he had seen him elsewhere known by the name of De Villon. He said it would invalidate the will; of course he was kind enough to explain to the lawyer what the law was on that point. They were both in a frightful wax."

Father Brown laughed. "People often are when they are to witness a will," he said; "for one thing, it means that they can't have any legacy under it. But what did Dr. Valentine say? No doubt the universal secretary knew more about the doctor's name than the doctor did. But even the doctor might have some information about his own name."

Fiennes paused a moment before he replied.

"Dr. Valentine took it in a curious way. Dr. Valentine is a curious man. His appearance is rather striking but very foreign. He is young but wears a beard cut square; and his face is very pale, dreadfully pale and dreadfully serious. His eyes have a sort of ache in them, as if he ought to wear glasses, or had given himself a headache with thinking; but he is quite handsome and always very formally dressed, with a top hat and a dark coat and a little red rosette. His manner is rather cold and haughty, and he has a way of staring at you which is very disconcerting. When thus charged with having changed his name, he merely stared like a sphinx and then said with a little laugh that he supposed Americans had no names to change. At that I think the colonel also got into a fuss and said all sorts of angry things to the doctor; all the more angry because of the doctor's pretensions to a future place in his family. But I shouldn't have thought much of that but for a few words that I happened to hear later, early in the afternoon of the tragedy. I don't want to make a lot of them, for they weren't the sort of words on which one would like, in the ordinary way, to play the eavesdropper. As I was passing out towards the front gate with my two companions and the dog, I heard voices which told me that Dr. Valentine and Miss Druce had withdrawn for a moment in the shadow of the house, in an angle behind a row of flowering plants, and were talking to each other in passionate whisperings—sometimes almost like hissings; for it was something of a lovers' quarrel as well as a lovers' tryst. Nobody repeats the sort of things they said for the most part; but in an unfortunate business like this I'm bound to say that there was repeated more than once a phrase about killing somebody. In fact, the girl seemed to be begging him not to kill somebody, or saying that no provocation could justify killing anybody; which seems an unusual sort of talk to address to a gentleman who has dropped in to tea."

"Do you know," asked the priest, "whether Dr. Valentine seemed to be very angry after the scene with the secretary and the colonel—I mean about witnessing the will?"

"By all accounts," replied the other, "he wasn't half so angry as the secretary was. It was the secretary who went away raging after witnessing the will."

"And now," said Father Brown, "what about the will itself?"

"The colonel was a very wealthy man, and his will was important. Traill wouldn't tell us the alteration at that stage, but I have since heard only this morning in fact—that most of the money was transferred from the son to the daughter. I told you that Druce was wild with my friend Donald over his dissipated hours."

"The question of motive has been rather overshadowed by the question of method," observed Father Brown thoughtfully. "At that moment, apparently, Miss Druce was the immediate gainer by the death."

"Good God! What a coldblooded way of talking," cried Fiennes, staring at him. "You don't really mean to hint that she—"

"Is she going to marry that Dr. Valentine?" asked the other.

"Some people are against it," answered his friend. "But he

is liked and respected in the place and is a skilled and devoted surgeon."

"So devoted a surgeon," said Father Brown, "that he had surgical instruments with him when he went to call on the young lady at teatime. For he must have used a lancet or something, and he never seems to have gone home."

Fiennes sprang to his feet and looked at him in a heat of inquiry. "You suggest he might have used the very same lancet—"

Father Brown shook his head. "All these suggestions are fancies just now," he said. "The problem is not who did it or what did it, but how it was done. We might find many men and even many tools—pins and shears and lancets. But how did a man get into the room? How did even a pin get into it?"

He was staring reflectively at the ceiling as he spoke, but as he said the last words his eye cocked in an alert fashion as if he had suddenly seen a curious fly on the ceiling.

"Well, what would you do about it?" asked the young man. "You have a lot of experience; what would you advise now?"

"I'm afraid I'm not much use," said Father Brown with a sigh. "I can't suggest very much without having ever been near the place or the people. For the moment you can only go on with local inquiries. I gather that your friend from the Indian police is more or less in charge of your inquiry down there. I should run down and see how he is getting on. See what he's been doing in the way of amateur detection. There may be news already."

As his guests, the biped and the quadruped, disappeared, Father Brown took up his pen and went back to his interrupted occupation of planning a course of lectures on the encyclical *Rerum Novarum*. The subject was a large one and he had to recast it more than once, so that he was somewhat similarly employed some two days later when the big black dog again came bounding into the room and sprawled all over him with enthusiasm and excitement. The master who followed the dog shared the excitement if not the enthusiasm. He had been excited in a less pleasant fashion, for his blue eyes seemed to start from his head and his eager face was even a little pale.

"You told me," he said abruptly and without preface, "to

find out what Harry Druce was doing. Do you know what he's done?"

The priest did not reply, and the young man went on in jerky tones:

"I'll tell you what he's done. He's killed himself."

Father Brown's lips moved only faintly, and there was nothing practical about what he was saying—nothing that has anything to do with this story or this world.

"You give me the creeps sometimes," said Fiennes. "Did you—did you expect this?"

"I thought it possible," said Father Brown; "that was why I asked you to go and see what he was doing. I hoped you might not be too late."

"It was I who found him," said Fiennes rather huskily. "It was the ugliest and most uncanny thing I ever knew. I went down that old garden again, and I knew there was something new and unnatural about it besides the murder. The flowers still tossed about in blue masses on each side of the black entrance into the old grey summerhouse; but to me the blue flowers looked like blue devils dancing before some dark cavern of the underworld. I looked all round, everything seemed to be in its ordinary place. But the queer notion grew on me that there was something wrong with the very shape of the sky. And then I saw what it was. The Rock of Fortune always rose in the background beyond the garden hedge and against the sea. The Rock of Fortune was gone."

Father Brown had lifted his head and was listening intently.

"It was as if a mountain had walked away out of a landscape or a moon fallen from the sky; though I knew, of course, that a touch at any time would have tipped the thing over. Something possessed me and I rushed down that garden path like the wind and went crashing through the hedge as if it were a spider's web. It was a thin hedge really, though its undisturbed trimness had made it serve all the purposes of a wall. On the shore I found the loose rock fallen from its pedestal; and poor Harry Druce lay like a wreck underneath it. One arm was thrown round it in a sort of embrace as if he had pulled it down on himself; and on the broad brown sands beside it, in large crazy lettering, he had scrawled the words: 'The Rock of Fortune falls on the Fool.' "

"It was the colonel's will that did that," observed Father Brown. "The young man had staked everything on profiting himself by Donald's disgrace, especially when his uncle sent for him on the same day as the lawyer, and welcomed him with so much warmth. Otherwise he was done; he'd lost his police job; he was beggared at Monte Carlo. And he killed himself when he found he'd killed his kinsman for nothing."

"Here, stop a minute!" cried the staring Fiennes. "You're going too fast for me."

"Talking about the will, by the way," continued Father Brown calmly, "before I forget it, or we go on to bigger things, there was a simple explanation, I think, of all that business about the doctor's name. I rather fancy I have heard both names before somewhere. The doctor is really a French nobleman with the title of the Marquis de Villon. But he is also an ardent republican and has abandoned his title and fallen back on the forgotten family surname. 'With your Citizen Riquetti you have puzzled Europe for ten days.' "

"What is that?" asked the young man blankly.

"Never mind," said the priest. "Nine times out of ten it is a rascally thing to change one's name; but this was a piece of fine fanaticism. That's the point of his sarcasm about Americans having no names—that is, no titles. Now in England the Marquis of Hartington is never called Mr. Hartington; but in France the Marquis de Villon is called M. de Villon. So it might well look like a change of name. As for the talk about killing, I fancy that also was a point of French etiquette. The doctor was talking about challenging Floyd to a duel, and the girl was trying to dissuade him."

"Oh, I *see*," cried Fiennes slowly. "Now I understand what she meant."

"And what is that about?" asked his companion, smiling.

"Well," said the young man, "it was something that happened to me just before I found that poor fellow's body; only the catastrophe drove it out of my head. I suppose it's hard to remember a little romantic idyll when you've just come on top of a tragedy. But as I went down the lanes leading to the colonel's old place I met his daughter walking with Dr. Valentine. She was in mourning, of course, and he always wore black as if he were going to a funeral; but I can't say that their faces were very funereal. Never have I seen two people looking in their own way more respectably radiant and cheerful. They stopped and saluted me, and then she told me they were married and living in a little house on the outskirts of the town, where the doctor was continuing his practice. This rather surprised me, because I knew that her old father's will had left her his property; and I hinted at it delicately by saying I was going along to her father's old place and had half expected to meet her there. But she only laughed and said: 'Oh, we've given up all that. My husband doesn't like heiresses.' And I discovered with some astonishment they really had insisted on restoring the property to poor Donald; so I hope he's had a healthy shock and will treat it sensibly. There was never much really the matter with him; he was very young and his father was not very wise. But it was in connection with that that she said something I didn't understand at the time; but now I'm sure it must be as you say. She said with a sort of sudden and splendid arrogance that was entirely altruistic:

" 'I hope it'll stop that redhaired fool from fussing any more about the will. Does he think my husband, who has given up a crest and a coronet as old as the crusades for his principles, would kill an old man in a summerhouse for a legacy like that?' Then she laughed again and said, 'My husband isn't killing anybody except in the way of business. Why, he didn't even ask his friends to call on the secretary.' Now, of course, I see what she meant."

"I see part of what she meant, of course," said Father Brown. "What did she mean exactly by the secretary fussing about the will?"

Fiennes smiled as he answered, "I wish you knew the secretary, Father Brown. It would be a joy to you to watch him make things hum, as he calls it. He made the house of mourning hum. He filled the funeral with all the snap and zip of the brightest sporting event. There was no holding him, after something had really happened. I've told you how he used to oversee the gardener as he did the garden, and how he instructed the lawyer in the law. Needless to say, he also in-structed the surgeon in the practice of surgery; and as the surgeon was Dr. Valentine, you may be sure it ended in accusing him of something worse than bad surgery. The secretary got it fixed in his red head that the doctor had committed the crime, and when the police arrived, he was perfectly sublime. Need I say that he became, on the spot, the greatest of all amateur detectives? Sherlock Holmes never towered over Scotland Yard with more titanic intellectual pride and scorn than Colonel Druce's private secretary over the police investigating Colonel Druce's death. I tell you it was a joy to see him. He strode about with an abstracted air, tossing his scarlet crest of hair and giving curt impatient replies. Of course it was his demeanor during these days that made Druce's daughter so wild with him. Of course he had a theory. It's just the sort of theory a man would have in a book; and Floyd is the sort of man who ought to be in a book. He'd be better fun and less bother in a book."

"What was his theory?" asked the other.

"Oh, it was full of pep," replied Fiennes gloomily. "It would have been glorious copy if it could have held together for ten minutes longer. He said the colonel was still alive when they found him in the summerhouse, and the doctor killed him with the surgical instrument on pretense of cutting the clothes."

"I see," said the priest. "I suppose he was lying flat on his face on the mud floor as a form of siesta."

"It's wonderful what hustle will do," continued his informant. "I believe Floyd would have got his great theory into the papers at any rate, and perhaps had the doctor attested, when all these things were blown sky high as if by dynamite by the discovery of that dead body lying under the Rock of Fortune. And that's what we come back to after all. I suppose the suicide is almost a confession. But nobody will ever know the whole story."

There was a silence, and then the priest said modestly: "I rather think I know the whole story."

Fiennes stared. "But look here," he cried, "how do you come to know the whole story, or to be sure it's the true story? You've been sitting here a hundred miles away writing a sermon; do you mean to tell me you really know what happened already? If you've really come to the end, where in the world do you begin? What started you off with your own story?"

Father Brown jumped up with a very unusual excitement and his first exclamation was like an explosion.

"The dog!" he cried. "The dog, of course! You had the whole story in your hands in the business of the dog on the beach, if you'd only noticed the dog properly."

Fiennes stared still more. "But you told me before that my feelings about the dog were all nonsense, and the dog had nothing to do with it."

"The dog had everything to do with it," said Father Brown, "as you'd have found out if you'd only treated the dog as a dog, and not as God Almighty judging the souls of men."

He paused in an embarrassed way for a moment, and then said, with a rather pathetic air of apology: "The truth is, I happen to be awfully fond of dogs. And it seemed to me that in all this lurid halo of dog superstitions nobody was really thinking about the poor dog at all. To begin with a small point, about his barking at the lawyer or growling at the secretary. You asked how I could guess things a hundred miles away; but honestly it's mostly to your credit, for you described people so well that I know the types. A man like Traill, who frowns usually and smiles suddenly, a man who fiddles with things, especially at his throat, is a nervous, easily embarrassed man. I shouldn't wonder if Floyd, the efficient secretary, is nervy and jumpy, too; those Yankee hustlers often are. Otherwise he wouldn't have cut his fingers on the shears and dropped them when he heard Janet Druce scream.

"Now, dogs hate nervous people. I don't know whether they make the dog nervous, too; or whether, being after all a brute, he is a bit of a bully; or whether his canine vanity (which is colossal) is simply offended at not being liked. But anyhow there was nothing in poor Nox protesting against those people, except that he disliked them for being afraid of him. Now, I know you're awfully clever, and nobody of sense sneers at cleverness. But I sometimes fancy, for instance, that you are too clever to understand animals. Sometimes you are too clever to understand men, especially when they act almost as simply as animals. Animals are very literal; they live in a world of truisms. Take this case: a dog barks at a man and a man runs away from a dog. Now, you do not seem to be quite simple enough to see the fact: that the dog barked because he disliked the man and the man fled because he was frightened of the dog. They had no other motives and they needed none; but you must read psychological mysteries into it and suppose the dog had supernormal vision, and was a mysterious mouthpiece of doom. You must suppose the man was running away, not from the dog but from the hangman. And yet, if you come to think of it, all this deeper psychology is exceedingly improbable. If the dog really could completely and consciously realize the murderer of his master he wouldn't stand yapping as he might at a curate of a teaparty; he's much more likely to fly at his throat. And on the other hand, do you really think a man who had hardened his heart to murder an old friend and then walk about smiling at the old friend's family, under the eyes of his old friend's daughter and postmortem doctor—do you think a man like that would be doubled up by mere remorse because a dog barked? He might feel the tragic irony of it; it might shake his soul, like any other tragic trifle. But he wouldn't rush madly the length of a garden to escape from the only witness whom he knew to be unable to talk. People have a panic like that when they are frightened, not of tragic ironies, but of teeth. The whole thing is simpler than you can understand.

"But when we come to that business by the seashore, things are much more interesting. As you stated them, they were much more puzzling. I didn't understand that tale of the dog going in and out of the water; it didn't seem to me a doggy thing to do. If Nox had been very much upset about something else, he might possibly have refused to go after the stick at all. He'd probably go off nosing in whatever direction he suspected the mischief. But when once a dog is actually chasing a thing, a stone or a stick or a rabbit, my experience is that he won't stop for anything but the most peremptory command, and not always for that. That he should turn round because his mood changed seems to me unthinkable."

"But he did turn round," insisted Fiennes, "and came back without the stick."

"He came back without the stick for the best reason in the world," replied the priest. "He came back because he couldn't find it. He whined because he couldn't find it. That's the sort of thing a dog really does whine about. A dog is a devil of a ritualist. He is as particular about the precise routine of a game as a child about the precise repetition of a fairy tale. In this case something had gone wrong with the game. He came back to complain seriously of the conduct of the stick. Never had such a thing happened before. Never had an eminent and distinguished dog been so treated by a rotten old walking stick."

"Why, what had the walking stick done?" inquired the young man.

"It had sunk," said Father Brown.

Fiennes said nothing, but continued to stare; and it was the priest who continued:

"It had sunk because it was not really a stick, but a rod of steel with a very thin shell of cane and a sharp point. In other words, it was a sword stick. I suppose a murderer never gets rid of a bloody weapon so oddly and yet so naturally as by throwing it into the sea for a retriever."

"I begin to see what you mean," admitted Fiennes; "but even if a sword stick was used, I have no guess of how it was used."

"I had a sort of guess," said Father Brown, "right at the beginning when you said the word summerhouse. And another when you said that Druce wore a white coat. As long as everybody was looking for a short dagger, nobody thought of it; but if we admit a rather long blade like a rapier, it's not so impossible."

He was leaning back, looking at the ceiling, and began like one going back to his own first thoughts and fundamentals.

"All that discussion about detective stories like the Yellow Room, about a man found dead in sealed chambers which no one could enter, does not apply to the present case, because it is a summerhouse. When we talk of a Yellow Room, or any room, we imply walls that are really homogeneous and impenetrable. But a summerhouse is not made like that; it is often made, as it was in this case, of closely interlaced but separate